THE BOOK KEEPER

SARAH PIN

 FriesenPress

One Printers Way
Altona, MB R0G 0B0
Canada

www.friesenpress.com

ISBN
978-1-03-914525-2 (Hardcover)
978-1-03-914524-5 (Paperback)
978-1-03-914526-9 (eBook)

1. YOUNG ADULT FICTION, ACTION & ADVENTURE

Distributed to the trade by The Ingram Book Company

THE BOOK KEEPER

MYSTERIOUS BOOKSHOPS CAN BE DISAPPOINTING

A lock turned.

A door opened.

Bells rung.

For the first time in much too long, someone entered the little bookshop. The dust that had been accumulating for months swirled through the air. The young woman looked around in awe.

The maze of bookshelves welcomed you to lose yourself in the many worlds where stories are told. The cold, dark fireplace encouraged you to light it and snuggle up in cozy warmth on the surrounding couches with your favourite book. An old vintage cash register sat on the front counter, ready to ring out someone's next adventure.

She took a deep breath and smelled the old books. A smile grew on her face.

My own little bookshop, she thought.

She sneezed, then waved a hand in front of her face as her sinuses filled up. The dust she'd kicked up had formed a haze in the shop. *Okay, it'll need a lot of dusting.*

The evening air wafted in once the front door was propped open with an umbrella stand, and some of the haze started to filter out.

In the meantime, she let herself get lost among the rows of books, her finger running along leather and paper spines. She was surprised by how many titles she recognized.

"Never Leave." A fantasy in which the father gets enlisted in the army, and the only thing that gets him through the bloody battles is the thought of returning home to his family with the promise to never leave them again.

"Young Magic." Those who possess abilities are of a higher social standing than everyone else, until one young wizard born to a non-magic family starts a rebellion against the magic counsel.

"Oh! Legend of Four Fires! I love these ones. And they're all here too. Aw, it's been ages since I read through them…"

She couldn't help herself. She pulled down Book One and brushed the dust from the cover, revealing a red dragon that was coiled around a floating flame. The book's first words welcomed her like an old friend.

Chapter 1

In a land ruled by nobles and threatened by the shadows, you would think that the best place to be is in the capital where you could spend all your days in the palace. You'd get the excitement of seeing the knights training for battle. You could listen into the strategists' meetings. Or even keep up with the gossip about love triangles and drama of the noblemen and women.

At least, that's what the stories all said.

Hi, I'm Anthony. Six months ago, I decided I was fed up with the simple life of a fisherman and set out to the capital where my life's adventure was destined to begin. Maybe I would join the army and win glory in battle. Or I'd catch the eye of a princess. Or maybe an artisan would see some kind of raw, hidden talent within me and take me on as an apprentice.

…So I like to dream. Mug me!

Needless to say, none of those things actually happened. I did manage to find work within the palace after weeks of looking and begging, but it isn't as glorious as I'd been led to believe. I've never seen a knight or a strategist, and definitely no one of high standing. No, all I ever see are the crotchety cooks and the servants who deliver the food to the dining hall, all the while scrubbing away at the ever-growing pile of dishes. If there's a break in the line of pots and platters, I have the pleasure of sweeping or polishing the silverware or dumping the scraps to the pigs… the list goes on. I hardly have a chance to eat, let alone divulge in castle gossip.

But everything was about to change.

One day, when I'm out feeding chicken bones and guts to the pigs, I see it shining in the mud. I set down my bucket and crouch down to get a better look. Sure enough, it glints in the sunlight. My fingers sink into the ground, and I grasp whatever is shining and bring a fistful of mud along with it. I wipe away the grime until a large green gem sits all dirty in my hand.

"Holy mother of—"

Poof! "Hello!"

"Agh!" I jump back and drop the gem as a little green fairy appears from a puff of smoke.

"Please," the sprite implores. "You must help us. You're the only one who can save my people."

In that moment, I knew my purpose.

"Chore boy!"

The angry yell from the cook brings me out of my fantasy, and I realize that the sink had overflowed with the last bucket of water I'd poured.

"Uhhh…"

"You stupid boy! Can't you do anything right?"

She smiled as the boy continued to fumble around and cause general havoc. Every cook in the kitchen was angry, except for ol' Harold, who simply laughed jovially and gave Anthony a pat on the back in silent encouragement.

Not long after this incident, Anthony gets fired for blowing up one of the kitchen's ovens. Then book's adventure truly starts when the capital is attacked. In the chaos, Anthony helps a young boy and girl escape from the city only to find out they're the prince and the next high priestess who must embark on a quest to find the four dragon fires that will help them take the kingdom back, but not without recruiting a few more allies on the way.

It's a heartwarming story of adventure and growth that she instantly took to when she first read it. She'd sped through the first four books before having to wait six agonising months for the conclusion to release. It was hard, but she'd persevered.

Her nose twitched and she snapped the book shut as she sneezed again.

"Ah, yes, more dust." She wiped her nose on her sleeve and returned the book to the shelf, then continued exploring.

The corner with the fireplace had seen better days. The soot was dark and old, and the couches reeked of mildew. The whole thing creaked when she kicked the leg.

"Okay, new couches." She eyed the gaudy floral pattern. "Not that anyone will miss them."

Pattering around to the front counter, she eyed the beautiful piece that sat proudly on of it: the cash register.

It was coated in bronze with coloured buttons and a big, crankable lever on the side. She brushed off a layer of grime from the display screen and pushed a few buttons. The little pings it made had her giggling in delight.

It still worked… for the most part.

She took the lever in hand and pulled. The machine jingled and the drawer popped but didn't open. Disappointed, she jiggled it. The drawer rattled, but something was jamming it.

"Oh well," she muttered to herself. "Problem for tomorrow. How cool would it be if I could still use it? I wonder if there's anything still inside?"

She jiggled it some more and shone her phone light towards it to see if she could see something blocking it. After a few minutes of tinkering with no luck, she gave up.

She sighed in defeat and turned to lean against the counter. That's when she noticed the old-looking, beautifully carved door that led to what must be the back room.

The tarnished brass knob turned with bit of resistance, but the door creaked open without any further prompting…

As if it had been waiting for someone to open it again, she mused.

A single shaft of light pierced through the darkness. If she thought the rest of the store was dusty, then the back room could kill a person. She could only see what the sliver of light revealed, but she could smell it even through her clogged nose.

"Geez." She grimaced as she felt around the wall for the light switch.

Something wispy met her touch instead. It wrapped around her fingers and stuck fast. She bit back a panicked screech and snatched her hand back. She shivered as she caught sight of what she'd touched.

Cobwebs.

Just cobwebs.

"Haaaaaaaa," she breathed out instead of swearing and took a minute to let her heart settle. With a shiver, she turned on her phone's flashlight again and shone it around until it landed on a single string dangling from the ceiling that connected to a lone, bare lightbulb.

"Really?" She pulled the string in annoyance, and it flickered on. The light was just bright enough to chase away the darkest shadows.

Cluttered. That was one word to describe the back room. A row of metal shelves took up most of the space and there was a long workbench along the opposite side that was just as cluttered as the rest of the room. Handwritten notes with diagrams and arrows had been thrown haphazardly on it. Some had complicated math equations, all of which were beyond her. It was her uncle's work.

She had only met her Uncle Ken once, and she'd been too young to remember anything from the visit. She never knew him, but she'd heard the stories.

Your uncle Ken is somewhat of an oddity, her father had told her. *He means well, but he'll go on these tangents about stuff that doesn't exist. At first, I thought he was only talking about his books, but he'd talk about these theories, and after a while, I had to wonder if it really was all in his head.*

His projects. They were all laid out before her now. No one could ever tell her what he had been working on. Looking at his workspace now, she still couldn't tell. It almost looked like he was building something, but she had no idea what it was. She wasn't an engineer; she was a business major. Well… emphasis on the *was*.

Uncle Ken was a mystery. The letter he had sent her had only produced more questions.

Dear Margaret,

I'm writing to you because I know I'm not long for this world. I have many regrets and even more things I wish I had done differently, but it's all in the past now and something you oughtn't worry about.

I wish we could have had the opportunity to know each other and share our stories, but I fear this letter won't reach you until it's too late. But don't mind that. It's what I'm leaving behind that concerns me.

He goes on to give her his life's work, the Book Portal. Whether she sells the property, opens the store back up, or just lets it sit to rot, he left the choice up to her. But he made one odd request.

"An antique Greek book, embroidered in gold," she whispered. "Whatever you choose, keep it safe."

He told her that it was so old that even opening it to turn the pages might damage it. Uncle Ken would have kept something so precious somewhere safe.

She stepped up to a bookcase with glass doors that was tucked beside the workbench. It held a number of colourful books. Scanning through them, they didn't seem special. They didn't even seem to have anything in common. She wondered why they were all stored back here. If it weren't for the number of children and young readers' books mixed in, she would have thought they were her uncle's private collection, or something along those lines. But it was as if he just chose a bunch of books off the shelves all willy-nilly and decided they would be kept back here.

Odd.

In any case, the antique Greek book that was embroidered in gold wasn't among them. She moved on.

She turned her attention to the rows of shelves. The shelving units that took up most of the back room were as cluttered as the rest of the space. She rifled through a few boxes, assuming they would be filled with more books that hadn't fit out on the shelves, but no. She gave up after boxes revealed only junk. Like, literal junk. Old, unopened boxes of food, ratty clothes, dirty kids' toys. Was Uncle Ken a hoarder?

"What kind of back room is this anyway?" she huffed, then brushed her hands off on her pants. It was more of a work room than a back room. You would think her uncle would have used the second-floor living area for his personal work since there was more room there.

Her footprints trailed deeper into the room where a simple dark wooden desk sat. It had two drawers on either side and was covered in clutter like everything else in this back room. She shuffled some of the clutter around and opened the overflowing drawers but still found nothing of interest.

She'd have to go through everything back here and get rid of a bunch of stuff. Looking around, she realized it was going to be a big, time-consuming job.

She tucked the little wooden chair back into place under the desk.

Thunk.

Huh?

She pulled it back out and slid it in again.

Thunk.

Something was under the desk.

She slid the chair out of the way and crouched down. The single bare lightbulb wasn't quite strong enough to shine light under the desk, so she felt around and pulled out a lockbox.

"Would you look at that." It was a plain metal fire-proof box with a pattern etched into it—a similar pattern to the one on the door to the back room.

She glanced over her shoulder to where the door was still open.

Definitely similar.

So, what does that mean? she mused, and a smile tugged at her face. She tilted the box and heard something shuffle inside. She shook it again and listened as if she would be able to tell what it was. Then she felt silly, so she stopped.

The small latch was stuck tight. The little keyhole was keeping whatever secrets it held nice and safe. Oh, what could they be?

A claim to riches? The deed to a foreign piece of land? A sinister plot that should never see the light of day?

She ran her finger over the keyhole and her thoughts went wild. Then she remembered the set of keys that had opened the shop. She pulled out the metal ring, and the handful of little keys jingled around. She eyed them and picked out which ones were most likely to fit.

That one opened the shop's front door. That one led to the apartment on the second floor. That one was to the cash safe under the register.

She tried some of the smaller keys first and after the third try, the very smallest key slid right in. The latched popped. The box seemed to sigh.

The anticipation rose as she slowly extended her arm, lifting the lid of the mysterious locked box that only *she* had the key for, inherited from her mysterious late uncle who she knew very little about.

What was inside?

Papers.

It—it was more papers. Bank statements, taxes, bills, lawyer stuff, sales records. Important stuff that should probably be kept locked up and out of sight.

The box clanged shut, and she kicked it back in its place. The desk rattled and a pile of clutter slid off like a waterfall, uncovering a brown leather-bound book with a Greek title woven in gold thread.

The book. The one her uncle wanted her to keep safe. The delicate *should-not-be-opened* book was just sitting right out in the open.

She picked it up and smacked it to her forehead. How anticlimactic was that?

Where's the adventure? Where's the suspense? The mystery?

But at least she'd found it.

"Aw, screw it," she muttered. The mood was shot. She placed the old book back where she had found it and rubbed her eyes. "I'll find a place for it tomorrow."

The string was pulled, the room plunged back into darkness, and the wooden door closed.

For now, she needed a good night's sleep and a heck of a lot of cleaning supplies. It was going to be a lot of work to get the shop ready to open again.

She left the old Greek book in the back room and locked the door on her way out.

CHAPTER 2

I TAKE IT BACK...

A week.

That's how long it took to get everything sorted out. After a tremendous amount of cleaning supplies, visits from a plumber and an electrician, meetings with bankers and lawyers, she was set to inherit the Book Portal. It would soon be ready to open.

The next thing to conquer was the mess.

The amount of grime on the shelves was worse than she'd thought. After a little research on how to properly maintain books, she started to systematically go through every book on every shelf. One at a time, the shelves were emptied, each book was wiped down with a special dusting cloth, then the shelf was cleaned of any dust and mysterious spots, and a final touch of lavender was rubbed into the wood to prevent future growth of mildew and mould. Once it was dry, the books were returned, and she moved onto the next shelf.

It was a long, tedious task, but she enjoyed every moment of it. The monotony of flipping through all the books, the lethargic scent of old paper, and being able to peek into the more interesting-looking ones—she could spend days in here. Well, she was going to be spending a lot longer than that now that she legally *owned* the place!

She giggled at the thought and rocked where she sat on the floor. All these books for her to enjoy! And she'd get to share them with others too!

Her stiff back reminded her how long she'd been sitting on the floor, and her stomach reminded her that it was lunch time. She got up, stretched, and locked the front door on her way out.

The day was warm and sunny, so she took to the sidewalk. The Book Portal was on the corner of Treebare Lane, tucked in beside a laundromat. She waved to the lone laundromat worker as she passed by. She'd chatted with him a few days ago, and he seemed pleasant enough but had quickly gone back to his newspaper.

Further down the street, she passed a very small park, a mostly empty strip mall, and a fancy gym that advertised self-defence classes and a shooting range! Not a place she'd ever go to, but cool. She wasn't sure what to make of it anyway. There were quite a few cars parked in front of the gym, so it must be doing well. Good for them.

Three blocks away from the Book Portal, she entered a cute little diner called the Chipped Mug and was led to a booth in the back corner. An older lady with greying blonde hair poured her a cup of coffee and took her order before retreating behind the counter where a group of teenagers were waiting for take-out.

Was there a high school nearby? She idly considered asking if they would let her put up some flyers around the school. A book sat unopened in front of her as she watched the students place their orders. The three boys were tall, and one of them was wearing a football jersey with silver stripes. The two girls were peppy with bouncy hair and cell phones glued to their hands. Somehow, they both managed to keep talking without interrupting the other.

Jocks and preps. She smiled as a story started conjuring in her mind.

Five teens find themselves lost in a disaster zone with no survivors. The city has been demolished by alien raids, and nothing but rubble remains. Together, they scavenged for food, built a shelter, and even found a weapons storage depot where they armed themselves for the next strike.

10

Dave is the leader. He's tall with dark brown hair and an easy smile. His time as star quarterback paid off when he and Alice went on a supply run and came across alien ground troops! He managed to single-handedly fight them off, and ever since, he and Alice began developing feelings that went a little farther than 'just friends.'

Harold is the engineer of the group. Not as tall, but equally handsome. In school, he bypassed sports in favour of studying physics. He showed his strength when he helped design their shelter and transform scrap metal and broken appliances into their new defence system and communication devices. He mostly kept to himself, except for when he was demonstrating his newest toys with a dramatic flare.

Alice and Trina have been BFFs since *forever*! But after the initial attack, they found that maybe they weren't as close as they'd originally thought. Ever since Alice and Dave became a thing, Trina found herself drifting even further from her so-called friend.

Finally, there's Carl, always the strong silent type. Never saying a word unless completely necessary. He often uses hand signals in favour of talking. No one knows why, but he's always been like that. He acts as their scout and lookout, scoping out the safe paths and keeping an eye on his fellow survivors.

She took a sip of her coffee and fiddled with the cover of her book. She was happy with her cast of characters. Now to get the story started. She let the bitter caffeine linger in her mouth before swallowing.

The door to the diner opened, and a second group of teens—three boys—came in with baggy clothes, chains around their necks, and shoes that kept falling off.

Hm…

After three months, they come across another group of survivors. Trina suggests they should all stick together and team up. Maybe they could try to find others and mount an attack against the alien invaders. Dave considers the idea, but Alice is weary of the newcomers. She's more concerned this new group is going to get them all killed instead of helping everyone. Harold thinks it's worth giving them a chance. Carl simply shrugs and casts his gaze toward the horizon, all cool like, and keeps a lookout for any aliens.

Drama arises between the two groups, and instead of coming together, they are driven apart. In the end, Trina feels betrayed by Alice and helps the new group raid their camp. She ends up running off with the new boys and taking all of Harold's technology and blueprints with her.

The group of preps got their food and left the diner with their takeout bags, still chatting away and paying the other group of boys no mind whatsoever.

In a dramatic conclusion, the alien invaders send an entire team to sweep the ruined city in search of survivors, and the two groups are forced together in their attempt to fight back. They confront each other and agree to work together to fight off the alien scum. They could go back to attacking each other after that.

The second group of boys placed their orders.

In a twist of fate, the two groups are separated once again when the aliens come out with a new weapon that teleports the original group to their space station where they will be experimented on and put through grueling tests to find the limits of human physical strength. The second group comes to realize the futility of fighting the aliens by themselves and begrudgingly agree that they must save the kidnapped humans.

The boys got their food and left the diner.

And so, they set out on a journey to save their rivals who had become more like comrades in their shared struggles. But will they succeed?

"Here you go, dear," the waitress pulled her from her daydream. A plate with a burger and fries was placed in front of her. "Sorry for the wait."

"Thank you." She smiled, snapping out of her dream. She should really stop doing that.

She opened the book in front of her.

The sun was setting, and the light retreated from the windows of the Book Portal. She stretched and felt her spine pop back into place. She sighed in relief.

Looking around, she was happy with what she'd managed to accomplish. The dust and grime was gone, the fireplace was cleaned out, you could actually see through the windows, and the smell of old mould was finally dispersing. Tomorrow, she'd finish going through all the shelves and maybe order a new set of couches. She still had to clean out the back room, but it wasn't high on her priority list. It's not like people would be going back there anyway.

Ready to call it a night, she headed to the set of stairs nestled in the back of the store. Passing by the counter with the old register, she noticed a book. It was the old Greek book her uncle had wanted her to keep safe. Was that where she had left it? She couldn't remember.

Maybe she'd grabbed it when the electrician had come over to install a new light in the back room?

Oh well. She shook her head. It was time to call it a day. She was halfway up the stairs when she heard something. It was like a high-pitched ringing. She stopped and listened. It sounded like a text tone but more annoying.

With a furrowed brow, she trudged back down to the shop. It was definitely coming from there. There wasn't some sort of alarm system, was there? She tilted her head and scanned the room. Her gaze fell on the Greek book that was sitting patiently beside the register.

She stared at the book. The sound was coming from it.

"What?" she huffed under her breath. A book was singing to her. A book was singing to her! What the heck? Was this for real? She wasn't daydreaming again, was she?

She looked around the shop as if someone would pop out and tell her that she was just hearing things. Instead, she remembered the final part of Uncle Ken's letter.

It is my hope that you will find your next adventure within the walls of the Book Portal, as I found mine.

A singing book sure sounded like an adventure to her, but then again, so did the lockbox she found under the desk, and that turned out to be a big disappointment.

But this was *real*. At least, she thought it was. She *hoped* it was.

Her heartbeat picked up and her breath caught as she reached out to touch the book. The ringing seemed to resonate as her hand got closer and the cover started vibrating. She touched the hardened brown leather, and the ringing suddenly stopped. The shop resonated in the sudden silence.

A gasp slipped from her lips as she felt the warmth under her fingers. Sliding her hand to the edge, she hooked a finger under the cover. One last pause to let the tension build, then…

She lifted the cover.

Light erupted from the book as it started to rise. A green haze spilled over the counter, the arc of light growing as the book opened further. The ringing started up again and grew in intensity.

Oh.

The excitement drained as she saw the first page. More specifically, what was *left* of the first page.

Someone had cut a hole into the pages to create a hiding spot. Inside was some sort of device with a green LED screen, its light spilling into the dark room. And it was ringing. The sound was suddenly a lot more irritating now than it was a few seconds ago.

It wasn't a magical book. Of course it wasn't a magical book. This was real life, not one of her fantasies. Then again, there was still a mysterious machine in an old Greek book that was making noises in her book shop. Maybe this was a sci-fi, not a fantasy?

She leaned closer to look at the device. It had a black plastic casing with wires and bits of metal welded on. Letters from different languages scrolled across the LED screen—more gibberish—and a couple of grey buttons. The temptation to play with them was there, but she didn't exactly want to break anything.

The ringing was starting to really grate on her nerves at this point. She turned the thing over in her hand to see if there was an ON/OFF switch. Instead, she found a little plastic panel and pried it off.

"Taking out the batteries works too." She shrugged and easily pulled them out. They weren't any brand she'd ever seen before. It was as if they had been made specifically for this device.

What *was* her uncle working on?

Thankfully, the ringing stopped, and the device went dark. She hummed in the now silent shop, held up the inactive device, and turned to lean against the counter.

She didn't see what happened to the book behind her. Finally free of that retched device, the old Greek book began to glow. The black ink on what remained of the pages shimmered with an ethereal green luminescence and shifted as if alive. The foreign words started to swirl around and around, glowing brighter and moving faster until they began lifting off the paper.

It was silent at first, but the vortex of words quickly gained speed. A green twister made of Greek symbols formed over the book.

The gradual tug of wind finally drew her attention from fantasizing about the device back to the book. Her eyes widened as she saw the storm that had formed inside her bookshop.

"Holy mother of—" She fell back flat on her butt with wide eyes and a gaping mouth. The mysterious device clattered to the ground beside her.

She could only watch, frozen and enthralled by the windstorm. She was daydreaming again. She had to be. The storm grew and the words whipped around and around, spinning so fast that at first, she didn't see the figure emerging from within.

A green haze billowed over the edge of the counter and a deep, maddening laughter echoed around the bookshelves. He rose from the windstorm. White hat, tipped with something metallic, a maddened grin peeking from behind its brim, dark hair tied back, and a long white coat full of pockets and tails that danced in the Greek wind.

"It worked! I'm finally free!"

The man stretched up to his full height on top of her counter. The vortex was suddenly swept away. The ink splashed back onto the pages and the letters settled in their proper places.

It was suddenly very quiet.

The man in the white coat rolled his neck and stretched his arms above his head, sighing as joints popped and cracked back into place. His gaze landed on the Greek book that was now sitting lifeless beneath his feet.

"Rotten thing," he cursed and kicked it across the room. Then he noticed the girl, watching petrified from her spot on the floor. "Oh, it seems I have an audience." The smile that spread across his face was mischievous. She felt something twang in her chest at the quirk of his lips, and she couldn't help but skitter back when he hopped off the counter and landed gracefully in front of her. "And what might your name be, my dear?"

CHAPTER 3

WHY ARE ALL THE MYSTERIOUS MEN SO ATTRACTIVE?

She stared at the man who had just emerged from a mini vortex in the middle of her bookshop. All she could do was blink. She wasn't sure if she was breathing. She wasn't even sure if she was awake!

The silence stretched as the man's question went unanswered. His hand was still extended toward her, and he quirked an unimpressed eyebrow when she didn't move. "Are you alright?"

"Oh, geez." She flinched and was knocked from her head back to the present. She scrambled back to her feet and found her senses, or what was left of them. The man in the white coat watched her silently. "Um…" She stared back, not sure where to go from there. "Hi?"

"Hello," the man answered with a polite smile.

She waited for something more but got nothing. "Right."

She turned abruptly and walked right out the front door. The man peeked from around a shelf and watched her through the display window with an amused smirk. She looked around the street, checked her cell phone, and slapped her face a few times for good measure.

Breathe.

Breathe!

Breathing is good. Close your eyes and…

She blindly felt for the door and waited for the bells to jingle as it closed behind her.

One… Two… Three… Four… Five!

She opened one eye, then the other, and the man in the white coat as nowhere to be seen. The store was empty and silent. No strange man, no strange book, no strange windstorms. She sighed and visibly sagged against one of the bookshelves.

"Feeling better?" The man popped out from behind said shelf.

A scream tore from her throat as she stumbled back into another shelf, almost toppling it over.

"I'll take that as a no," the man replied with half-lidded eyes. He didn't offer to help her steady the shelf. "Pity. I do prefer it when my company responds with full sentences."

"You just—you're gonna have to give me a—give me a minute," she managed. Her heart was pounding, and it was hard for her to get a full breath.

"Take all the time you need." He waved her off and began running a finger along the lines of books. "When you're trapped in a book about Greek grammar for who knows how long, you tend to learn the art of patience."

"Trapped in—yeah. Sure. Naturally." She tried catching her breath. His babbling washed over her, and she watched him cautiously as he moved through the rows of books. He was clearly looking for something.

"You wouldn't happen to know where the children's books are kept, would you?" he asked suddenly. "Things seem to have changed since I was last here."

"You've been here?"

"Hm? Oh yes, yes. Now, the books?"

"Uh, over there, I think." She pointed towards the front of the store.

"You think?" he asked, not impressed, but continued over anyway. The section of shelves was only waist high—the perfect height for little ones to look through.

"I'm re-opening the shop," her voice wavered as she explained, though she didn't know why she was explaining herself to this strange man. "I'm still cleaning and getting ready, though…"

"Oh, didn't know it had closed."

"Uh, yeah. About a year ago. Who are you again?"

"Who, me?"

"No one else here."

"The books are here." He grinned. Cheeky.

"Books aren't people."

"No, but they contain people. And they often have much more to tell than the average human does."

"I totally agree," she nodded, confused but losing her sense of unease, "but you haven't answered my question. Who *are* you?"

"Hmm. Well, that's a tricky question."

"Are you ever going to give me a straight answer?"

"Should I?"

"Well, seeing that you came here, into *my* shop, out of nowhere, and from some magic vortex or something—although I'm still debating whether that was real or not—yes. Yes, I think you do owe me some sort of explanation."

"My apologies, my dear." The man in the white coat smiled over his shoulder before going back to scanning the children's books. "I suppose an explanation is in order. But where to begin? It's always tricky, figuring out where to begin a story."

"At the beginning is usually good."

"No, not always," the man replied cryptically. "Some things are better told through flashbacks or plot twists that further reveal the backstory."

"Perhaps if this was a book we were talking about," she agreed. "But this is a straightforward question that you keep trying to skirt around."

He sighed in resignation. "I won't bore you with the details. I've been called a great number of things. Names mean very little to me. Call me what you wish."

"I wasn't asking for your name. I was asking *who* you are."

"My, my." He turned and looked at her in a new light. "I like a human who asks the right questions. Alright then." He turned back to the shelf and extracted a random book. "Let me *show you* who I am."

He held out the book, and she hesitated before taking it. "*Space Norman Meets the Martians*," she read. Her eyebrows rose at the cutesy image of a young boy wearing a silver space suit and standing beside green aliens on a red planet.

Before she could say anything else, he pulled up the sleeve of his white coat and started fiddling with an overly complicated bracelet thing that looked like it came right out of a steampunk novel. Complex gears and overlapping metal bits shifted as he pressed invisible buttons.

It started humming and flashing green—the same green glow the Greek book had emitted when the man in the white coat had appeared. She didn't have time to decipher what it all meant before the book in her hands resonated with the bracelet and started glowing green too.

The book opened itself to a random page. She watched as the words became fluid. They started to slide along the paper, spinning faster and faster until they lifted off the page and another green vortex formed above the book in her hands.

The book clattered to the ground as she snatched her hands back and stumbled away from the storm. She bumped into the man, and he grabbed her shoulder to steady her. That same mad grin spread across his face as his coat swam in the howling winds.

All at once, they were sucked in.

■—■—■—■□■—■—■—■

"Open your eyes, my dear."

She shook her head. She was dreaming. She had to be. There was no way some crazy guy in a white coat came out of an old Greek book and then made a magical portal that sucked her into a different book.

"Come now, you're the one who wanted to know who I was," he tried provoking her.

"I didn't ask for a demonstration!"

"You wouldn't have believed me otherwise."

"You came out of a glowing green twister that magically formed on my counter."

"I can assure you that there was no magic involved," his voice went flat.

"Then what do you call *that*!" She finally opened her eyes and pointed aggressively out the window. His gaze flicked to the vast expanse of space riddled with millions of stars and the red, dusty planet of Mars that they were currently orbiting.

"Space has always existed."

"We were in a bookshop a minute ago, and now we're in a space shuttle piloted by an eight-year-old flying around Mars!"

"It could be dancing a tango and commanding an army of rocks, and it wouldn't be magic unless the author intended it to be magic."

"What are you talking about?" Her lips quivered, and she felt the sting of frustrated tears in her eyes.

"I'm talking about Space Norman." The man in the white coat smiled and waved at the child who was piloting the space shuttle. The kid smiled and waved back. "We're inside the book."

"I got that much! Thanks, Sherlock!"

"No, no, that's a different book."

"I'm gonna hit you!"

"Whatever you say, my dear."

She braced her arms against the windowsill and tried to compose herself. The infinite galaxy that was space met her gaze. It seemed so much closer here than it had anywhere she'd been to before. She watched as Mars circled below them, slowly getting closer.

"Coming in for a landing," Space Norman announced in his little-boy voice. He flipped switches and pushed buttons without hesitation as if an eight-year-old child could really fly a spaceship.

The craft landed with barely a bump, and Space Norman pulled on his space suit and went out to explore. She followed his movements through the window as he made footprints in the red sand. He turned to wave at them once more before bouncing off in the low gravity.

"You're being very quiet."

"How is this possible?"

"Science, of a sort." He brandished his weird bracelet thing, showing off its intricacies. "Long ago, I created this Portal Generator. It let me jump between planes of existence, and I had many adventures, learning and expanding my knowledge of the multiverse through my travels. Then one day, I discovered a different *type* of reality. One that is not as limited as the real world."

"Books?"

"Fictional worlds," he clarified. That mad grin was back. "Created by authors and limited only by their imaginations. When you put pen to paper and begin to create, a new world is born, so to say. A world that obeys all the laws that the author puts in place. If the author wants an eight-year-old boy to fly a spacecraft, then an eight-year-old boy can fly a spacecraft."

"Oh, my gosh." She gripped the window tighter and braced herself. Her heart was racing at the thought of all the stories she'd read through. Characters she would love to meet. Places she would love to see. Powers she would love to try out! She opened her eyes and realized her hands were trembling.

"Interested?" he asked, leaning casually against the wall beside her with a smirk on his face.

"In what?"

"Joining me on an adventure."

"What sort of adventure?"

"Any kind you wish."

Her breath caught in her throat. This was too good to be true. "Why?"

"Pardon?"

"Why me? Why would you want me on one of your adventures?"

"Well, you did help me. It's the least I can do."

"I did?"

"Yes. You remember that little box you found in the book I was trapped in?"

"Uh… the one that was ringing? Yeah."

"That little box was preventing me from escaping. It was, how do I put this, blocking my portal back to reality. When you deactivated it, I was able to open the gateway back to the bookshop."

"So, you're asking me on an adventure because I set you free?"

"That, and after so long with only the conjugation of Greek verbs to keep me company, someone who can respond to my ramblings would be a nice change."

She considered it for a moment. "Well, a mysterious man whisking me away to Mars is as good a start to an adventure as any." She smiled nervously.

"Well, then, my dear." He held out his hand to her. "Shall we?"

She placed her hand on top of his and grinned back. "We shall."

A smile reappeared on his face, and madness glinted in his eyes. "Didn't take much to convince you."

"I've been dreaming about adventures since I picked up my first book."

"Seeing as how you own a bookshop, I'd say we have a lot of ground to cover. So," he leaned in a little closer, and his grin morphed into a confident smirk, "let's get started."

He pulled back his sleeve and activated the Portal Generator. The vortex of swirling green words appeared out of thin air, and he led the way through without hesitation. She squeezed her eyes shut and only opened them when the man in the white coat loosened his hold on her hand. They were back in the Book Portal.

On the ground in front of her was *Space Norman Meets the Martians*. She bent down to pick it up. Suddenly, it didn't seem so childish anymore.

"I haven't read *Space Norman* since I was in fourth grade," she said, brushing the cover fondly.

"Well, now you've been to space," the man in the white coat said. He was back to combing through the shelves of children's books. "Mars even! What other human can say that?"

"Not like anyone will believe me." She slipped the book back onto the shelf.

The man paused for a split second. "What does the opinion of a random stranger mean to one who can transcend space?"

"What does it mean to transcend space if there's no one who'll believe your stories?"

He glanced over his shoulder. "Why do they need to believe it? Why can't it be just another fictional story?"

"Just another book in this vast library?"

"You have a response to everything, don't you?" His smile was amused, and he went back to looking through the books.

"I have too much time to myself to think."

"I love those times! No annoying people to interrupt a good train of thought."

"No one to share those thoughts with either."

He stopped to look at her with a raised eyebrow.

"Too much time thinking," she shrugged.

"So it seems. Well, my dear, now you have me to do all the thinking for you. Ah! Here it is!" He plucked another small chapter book from the shelf and flitted over to the front counter. She trailed after him and leaned against the opposite side with the book displayed between them. She read the title.

"*Mecha Arms Fighter: Heinsrick's Vengeance*! Sounds menacing."

"I am a little more invested in this one." He traced the edges of the book carefully. There was mischief in his eyes again.

"How so?"

"*Space Norman* was just a random book. Purely a demonstration to amaze you and buy time before you kicked me out or called the authorities."

"Oh, really?"

"Worked splendidly. But this one, on the other hand," he tapped the book, "I have visited before. Back before I was trapped in that Greek nightmare, I was travelling between fictional worlds, planting *seeds*, if you will."

"Carrot seeds?"

"What—no! Not *actual* seeds. More like a program. I set them off in different books to find each world's Print."

"And a Print is…?"

His eye twitched fractionally, almost annoyed at the interruption. "A Print exists within every fictional world. No matter how small or how large, there is *always* a Print hidden somewhere within the world's confines. The exact nature of it still eludes me, but from what I have gathered through my studies, a Print is something left behind by the one who created the world."

"You mean the author."

"Correct. As an author writes, a world is created in its own pocket dimension in the image of what the author imagines within their mind.

24

As such, a residue is left engraved, or *printed*, if you will, in that world. It appears in the form of what the author is most connected to in that world."

"So, what's so special about it?"

"For a long time, I believed that it simply existed. But it was only recently that I found that it did *much* more than that. I believe that it maintains the fictional world. Holds it in place, keeps it running, etc. It's basically the memory file that the world draws on to keep everything behaving as it should. It makes sure everything happens as the author wishes. Without it, the world would cease to exist."

"So, it's like the core?"

"In simpler words, yes."

"And you're searching for the Prints in order to… what? Study them? For what purpose?"

"What other purpose is there for research other than to under-stand something?"

"Usually, there's a benefit to humanity—some way to help advance mankind."

"My dear, I no longer live amongst mankind. I conduct my research for my own gains. I have no desire to walk alongside others in the real world."

"So, research for the sake of research? I guess I can get behind that."

"I'm glad you see things my way." He grinned madly. "Now, another thing that must be addressed is the matter of transportation."

"Transportation? Won't we just use your bracelet?"

His eye twitched. "Portal Generator," he corrected. "And yes, we will. But one Generator can only do so much. If you try transporting more than one person for more than, oh, say, three trips at a time, it will start to over-load. If you pass the threshold, then there's no guarantee that you'll make it through the vortex to your destination in one piece."

She hadn't been able to get a good look at the inside of the poral, but she was sure that however beautiful or terrifying it looked, it wasn't someplace she would want to get stuck.

"Right then," she swallowed the lump in her throat. "What do we do? Can you make another one?"

"No need," he flourished and spun to look around the shop. "The old man had my spare. It should be around here somewhere."

"Old man?"

"Yes, that old brute who used to run this shop. Since you're here now, I assume he's gone? Good riddance."

"You knew my Uncle Ken?"

"Uncle? Good god, you were related to him?"

"Uh, yeah. I—I never knew him."

"Then count yourself lucky." He leaned against the counter. By the way his shoulders had tensed up, she could tell there was more to the story.

"Why? Was he that bad? My dad always told me there was something off about Uncle Ken, but he would just brush it off, saying that he read too many books."

"He did more than just read them."

"You mean..."

"We were partners. We discovered the existence of the Prints together and hypothesized about them. But that was before he showed his true colours." His voice was set in a controlled pitch, but there was bitterness laced in his words.

"What do you mean?"

"I have a question of my own to ask you first, my dear."

"Uh, okay?"

"How do you think I came to be trapped inside an old book?"

"I... I don't know. It's not like a grammar book is fiction. Is that even a world you can travel to?"

"It's not really a fleshed-out world. More like an existence of only facts that are shoved into your brain at every second of every day. But that's beside the point. I didn't just decide to take a trip inside a book about a dead language one day and then just so happen to get stuck there. I was tricked into that book, and a device was set in place to make sure I stayed there."

"You mean, Uncle Ken did that?"

His gaze grew distant as he remembered the past. "He feared the unknown. I didn't realize what he was thinking until it was too late. I trusted him, and he ran off with my Portal Generator, leaving me to rot in a prison of alphas and deltas. Betrayal cuts deeper the more you trust."

Betrayal.

She knew that feeling too well. The reason her college life came to a crushing end. The reason she cut off all contact with those she *thought* were her friends. The same reason she moved away from everything she'd known to start anew.

She took those feelings and tried to picture the man she'd only seen in old photographs. Her uncle had always looked like a kind man with greying hair, thick glasses, and a big smile. She thought he'd be the kind of man who was always ready to help you pick out the perfect book.

Then again, Dad had always said he was spacey. He never quite knew what his brother was thinking. Now, the memory of Ken's smile blended with that of her old friends.

She'd never known the man personally. Maybe it was better that way. But why would he leave the shop to her? And what about his letter? Why would he want her to keep the Greek book safe? Or was he hoping that the one he'd wronged would be set free on his deathbed? Was he hoping for some sort of redemption for his past mistakes?

At this point, no one could answer those questions. The man was dead.

Then there was the man in the white coat. The one who had been betrayed, released from his prison, and took her into space. He was watching her expectantly, waiting for her response. She didn't know what he wanted to hear.

"Then what do you think of me?" she asked in a small voice.

"What's there to think about?" he answered. His stare was intense. She couldn't hold his eye.

"You learn that the person you just asked to come with you is related to the man you'd call your enemy, and you have nothing to say about it?"

"Lout's dead, isn't he? There's not much else he can do to me now."

"And so?"

"And so he has nothing to do with you. I say we find the Portal Generator he stole from me and make our own story. Why should we be held back by the past? Only the future holds the answers to things undiscovered."

Yes.

Yes!

That's exactly what she needed. Forget about the past, forget about people you couldn't trust, and stride forward with confidence.

"There's a bunch of boxes full of Uncle Ken's old things in the back room. I haven't been able to go through all of it yet. Your Portal Generator may still be kicking around."

"Brilliant! Then let's get—" He was interrupted by a beeping noise. His own Portal Generator flashed a mean red, and he yanked up his sleeve and cursed at whatever he saw.

"What is it?"

"Remember those seeds I told you about?"

"The programs? To find the Prints?"

"Yes, well, they found it all right. But a little snag has occurred. I am sorry, my dear, but I really must take care of this. In the meantime, try to find that other Portal Generator. It looks like this one." He flashed his shiny watch at her before he started pushing buttons again. "I'll explain how to activate it and everything once I return. I shouldn't be gone long."

He opened the *Mecha Arms Fighter* book to a seemingly random page and pushed one last button.

She watched as, once again, the letters on the page glowed green and started shifting. They swirled around the page, then lifted off, spinning faster and faster until the green vortex of a portal was opened on her counter.

The man in the white coat jumped up on a stool and stepped onto the counter. Just as he was about to jump in, he paused and turned back to her. His long ponytail blew about, and his silhouette was framed by the unearthly green glow. "I'm terribly sorry, my dear, but I don't believe I ever got your name."

She felt her breath leave her body, then smirked at him. "Aren't names fleeting?"

"Huh," he laughed. "I suppose they are."

"Margaret."

"Well, Margaret, my dear," he bowed deeply to her, "'till we meet again."

A flash, and the man disappeared. The portal snapped shut and everything was quiet. Everything was normal.

Margaret stood there staring at nothing for probably a good five minutes before she took a deep breath, climbed the stairs, and rolled right into bed.

Maybe things would make sense in the morning.

CHAPTER 4

OVERTHINKING THINGS, ODDLY ENOUGH, DOESN'T ACTUALLY HELP

*K*a-cha.

She stapled a flyer to the telephone pole and continued walking down the street.

Tall.

He had been tall. And quite pretty. Smooth skin. Crooked smile. Ponytail.

Ka-cha.

What book was he from again? She couldn't remember. It'd been a while since she read anything steampunk. A man travelling through dimensions, determined to learn, and a devastating betrayal.

It had been a book... right?

Because it would be crazy if some *guy* just—just popped out of a book. Even crazier for her to be in *space* a few minutes later.

Ka... cha.

She sighed and let the stapler fall to her side. Her flier was crooked. She glared at it. It didn't fix itself.

It had been a week since she woke up questioning reality. Thoughts of a man in a white coat filled her head as she went about her work. She disputed with herself as she got rid of the last traces of dust in the shop, convinced herself she was crazy as she picked out a new set of couches, and pushed any and all thoughts of him away as she got hold of some firewood for those chillier nights, but it all came crashing right back when she got around to repainting the sign hanging out front.

All in all, the shop looked amazing! The windows sparkled, the floor glistened, and she was no more certain about what happened that night than she had been a week ago. But hey, at least she was about ready to open! Well... except for the back room.

'The old man had my spare. It should be around here somewhere.'

Nope. There was absolutely no particular reason that she was avoiding the back room. It only had boxes of her uncle's personal belongings and, you know, *proof* of whether that night had actually happened or not...

The only time she'd gone back there was to let the electrician install an *actual* light. The excuse she was telling herself was that the customers don't see back there, so there was no need to prioritize cleaning it out.

The truth was that she was terrified.

Sure, the idea of travelling through different worlds with a complete stranger who just so happened to hate her late uncle, who coincidentally was the one who trapped said stranger inside a grammar book and stole his fancy watch, all sounded fine and dandy, but she was honestly about to have a mental breakdown here.

It had been days, and there was still no sign of the man in the white coat.

Still... she kept the book he'd disappeared into behind the counter, barely daring to touch it, just in case.

"Who am I kidding, I've completely lost it." She rubbed her eyes and left the flyer hanging crooked. *"But having common sense is so boring,"* she mumbled to herself in his proper way of speaking. *"You worry about the wrong things, my dear. Now that you have me, you'll have want to worry about."*

She stopped her mumbling. "'Want to worry about.' What's that supposed to mean? You can't just slap some words together and pretend it's gonna make sense."

Ugh.

Ka-cha.

She'd named him too, because although he didn't seem to care about names, they *did* mean something. He said to call him whatever she wanted. She couldn't just go around calling him 'The Man in the White Coat.' It was too much of a mouthful. Although coming up with something else hadn't been easy.

She couldn't just go with something normal like Mark, Jack, or Omar. He was too sophisticated to just smash letters on a keyboard and add vowels. Wrong genre to refer to him as something like Portal Man or Book Master—

Hm. *Book Master.* Master of the Books.

Fitting, but kind of long. A little too formal. What about…

It had been the middle of the night, but she threw the words into Google Translate to see what that would get. But where to start?

Greek? Seemed fitting enough…

Ah yes. Κύριος των βιβλίων. She knew *exactly* how to pronounce that! . . . So, no Greek.

She tried a couple of other languages for the heck of it. Spanish, Italian, Japanese —nothing seemed fit right.

French? The language of love?

Okay—wait, not like—no one said anything about that! She shook her head and felt her cheeks heat up at the thought. *It's not like that!* Or at least she told herself that. His dumb smirk flashed in her mind.

Maître des Livres.

Maître Livres? Livres, Maître? Maître. The Master. Master Maître of the Books.

It was cheesy but she found herself smiling as the name danced around her thoughts, and the 'r' rolled like a true Frenchman. The fancy hat on the 'i' also suited him.

Ka—

"Huh?" she squeezed the stapler again.

Ka—

She sighed. Out of staples.

■—■—■—■○■—■—■—■

Clak clak clak clak clak...

Work, work, work.

She typed away at her laptop, meticulously creating a catalogue using a program her brother made as part of a school project. All she had to do was enter each book manually... Yeah, she'd given herself another overly ambitious project that would take a *lot* of time to finish. But here she was, sipping on lukewarm coffee and totally not avoiding... other jobs.

She caught herself peeking at the carved wooden door behind her and forced her eyes back to her laptop. It was still a mess in there. And the Portal Generator that was supposedly hiding somewhere in her uncle's collection nagged at her.

Had it been real? Was *he* real?

All she had to do was look for it, and she'd have her answer. Her heart beat faster just thinking about it.

She slumped onto the counter and groaned.

Store's opening in a few days. I've got work to do. Don't have time to indulge in another fantasy.

She eyed the stack of books sitting beside her. The children's books had seemed like the only logical place to start. Now one of them sat apart from the others.

Mecha Arms Fighter: Heinsrick's Vengeance. The book he had disappeared into.

That night flashed through her mind again: looking out the window into the endless mass of stars, a mysterious man in a white coat extending his hand out to her with a smile that invited madness, and an eight-year-old child waving at her as he put on his spacesuit and ventured out onto the red planet.

It was an impossible experience. A fantasy. Pure fiction. A messed-up dream that was the result of the combined stress of trying to start a new life and moving to a new town and—

This is reality, Margaret. Wake up!

She turned away from the back room and slid the offending book out of sight.

"Real life comes first," she told herself aloud.

"*Since when*?" she imagined him saying. She could just *see* his grin challenging her to believe.

"Well," she spun on her stool, "can't argue with that!"

Before she could think, the beautifully carved door to the back room was flung open.

The door knocked against the wall, and everything became eerily silent. A haze of dust filtered through the air. She could still make out her footprints from the last time she set foot in there. She hadn't even gone in with the electrician.

Suddenly, it was a lot harder to move.

The newly installed light switch was stiff and made an audible *click* as she flipped it. The room looked a lot different in full lighting. The shadows and unease were chased away, and the very cluttered, still very dusty room didn't seem daunting anymore. It was just a room with rows and rows of shelves. It was the only place left with memories of her Uncle Ken, all still untouched.

"If I were a teleportation bracelet," she spoke to the air, "where would I hide?"

She let her feet wander and started shuffling stuff around on the workbench—mostly papers and little tools that had been left out. The wall above the bench was also covered in papers showing diagrams, mind maps, and point-form notes. The ink was fading, and some had fallen from the wall and lay in the scattered mess on the workbench.

There were a few boxes tucked underneath. She pulled one out, but it only had some books in it—stock that never made it out onto the floor. Another box held supplies: pens, printer paper, colourful sticky notes, ink cartridges.

Revisiting the desk at the back of the room was no better. She made sure to check under all the papers and stacked them in a pile as she went. Even in full lighting, she couldn't make out the gibberish writing. Did it have to do with the Portal Generator? Or Maître? Was there some record of their adventures together through the fictional worlds?

Now there's a story I'd read.

She sat in the chair and mindlessly kicked the lockbox underneath before going through the desk's drawers. The top one had more office supplies, and the bottom had some file folders. She riffled through them for the heck of it but was startled when her finger brushed against cold metal. She opened the drawer further and found a small revolver sitting there.

"What?"

She'd never held a gun before. It was heavier than she thought it would be. And colder. Really cold. She turned it over in her hands and watched as the fluorescent light reflected off the sleek barrel. She slid her finger over the trigger and pointed it at the wall. It felt big in her hand.

Did Uncle Ken bring this with him when he used the Portal Generator? She felt its weight. *Did he ever use it? Did he kill anyone? Did he try to kill Maître?*

Suddenly, she didn't feel so adventurous anymore. The gun fell back into the drawer, and she slammed it shut. Her hand shook slightly as she raked her hair out of her eyes and leaned back in the chair. There was so much she didn't know, and it was *not* reassuring.

Uncle Ken really was the bad guy, wasn't he?

She looked over her shoulder to where she could see the front counter through the open doorway. Her work was still waiting for her out there—a more ordinary day without mysterious, slightly attractive men coming out of books, and no guns in her uncle's desk.

"What are you doing, Margaret?" She let her head fall back and looked at the ceiling. "Always dreamed of the day your imagination would get the better of you. Didn't think it would actually happen…"

She glanced at all the shelves that were stacked with boxes and knick-knacks and sighed heavily again. "I've already made it this far," she grunted and swung to her feet again. "Might as well look for the stupid thing."

She started digging through boxes, letting things fall to the floor and clank around. The first couple of boxes held more office supplies, loose papers, and what she assumed were research notes. As she reached higher and higher on the shelves, the things she started pulling out got odder and odder.

The one that first threw her off was a box of clothes. She pulled out a shirt that felt like it was made of hay, all stiff and scratchy and smelling like dirt and sweat. She turned away from the smell and let the shirt drop to the ground. She pulled out a matching pair of trousers that didn't even have pockets. The rest of the box was filled with similar clothes that looked like they came from some poor village from medieval times.

She piled everything back in, leaving the questions for later.

The next box contained all sorts of wooden carvings ranging from animals to trees and people. Some had weird lines and symbols. The wood varied too: light or heavy, bright or faded, pure black to vibrant red.

At the bottom of that box were all sorts of coins. Different sizes, metals, designs. Some had holes in the middle, cog-like ridges, and heck, one was even made of stone!

"It's like a bunch of souvenirs," she mumbled, closing the box and wiggling it back in place. *Maybe because it is! Holy crap!* It was the stuff Uncle Ken must have brought back from his travels through fictional worlds! Or so she hoped.

She looked around with a new appreciation.

There were a few bulkier objects on one of the top shelves. She squinted and pulled the desk chair over. She was barely able to reach but managed to grab a wooden handle and haul one of the bigger things down. Stuff clattered to the ground around her, and the thing swung down, heavier than she expected. Her grip slipped, and she tumbled from the chair in a loud crash of metal and wood.

"Ow," she whined and glared at the offending object. But when she saw what it actually was, she forgot her bruises and began fawning over it. It was a crossbow. A long, wooden, *heavy* crossbow. "Sweet cherry-loving cheese."

She crossed her legs and dragged the weapon into her lap. She stroked the smooth wood and traced the metal ridging. Looking around, she found the bolts had scattered on the floor with some other stuff. She grabbed one and turned it over in her hand. It was sturdy, and the point was still sharp even after sitting on a shelf for who knows how long.

She was intrigued by the ancient weapon but was frightened by a gun. Odd, since they did the same thing. The only difference was the time period in which they were used.

A rustle from the store front pulled her from her thoughts. The whistle of wind building up and starting to spin. It sounded like a vortex beginning to form! She whipped her head around and saw the tell-tale green glow bleeding into the back room.

"He's back," she whispered, stunned. *It's real. It's all real!*

She scrambled to her feet and lunged for the door, toting the crossbow behind her. She stopped in the doorway and watched as *Mecha Arms Fighter* snapped open of its own accord. The text on the pages glowed green and swirled around the page. The words picked up speed and peeled off the paper. The vortex ragged in the middle of the shop. The wind whipped her hair around and howled in excitement.

Then someone stepped out onto the counter.

It wasn't him.

Her face contorted with confusion. It was a kid. He stood tall on the counter with shaggy black hair and dark clothes. Some sort of sash covered in what looked like shotgun shells was strapped across his chest, and on his back was a long mechanical cylinder that she swore was some sort of futuristic canon. Two more oversized guns were strapped to his arms. She looked at him again, and it clicked. She recognized him from the cover of the book.

"You're—"

"Nya ha ha ha ha!" he laughed. His eyes shone as he spread his arms wide in glee. "I've made it! A whole new world to plot against!"

"Uh…" She stood in the doorway. The colour was gone from her face. This was *not* how she imagined the reunion going. Especially since the guy who had come out of the book was a *character* from said book. More specifically, he was the villain who was always trying to destroy the world.

His eyes slid from the ceiling that he was laughing at to her. "Oh, look, my first witness!" he sang and pointed one of his futuristic guns at her. She flinched back. "You can be the one who tells stories about my victory. And oh, what a story it will be! After months of planning and endless work, teaming up with that weirdo with the white coat and stealing his device, I have not only found a way to conquer my own world, *but every other world in existence!* My name will ring throughout the multiverse, and everyone will fear Tidus Heinsrick!"

"Think again, dirt nugget!"

"What?" Heinsrick's eyes went wide at the new voice, and he turned towards the portal. "Impossible!"

"Next time, try closing the door on your way out." Another kid stepped out of the vortex, a confident smirk on his face, and he faced off against the villain. His weapon of choice was a set of robotic arms that were as long as he was tall and glinted red in the glow of the green vortex.

"Mecha Arms! You always find a way to throw a wrench in my plans," Heinsrick growled and levelled one of his arm guns at the kid.

"I've got more than a wrench." The hero pounded his robotic fists together.

"Do you really think your puny arms can stand up to the power of my *plasma*?"

"Let's put it to the test."

Heinsrick pulled the trigger on his guns and the barrels began to glow with an eerie blue light. The hero powered up his arms, and pulses of energy spread through them.

Then they both started yelling. They were just standing there, screaming at each other while their weapons powered up.

"AAAAAAAHHHHHHHHHH!"

"Plasma Canon!"

"Arming Fist!"

They leapt toward each other, and the weapons collided in a crash of light and energy. It was so intense that she had to cover her eyes and turn away.

Then... nothing?

The guns went cold and dark. The arms were suddenly too heavy to hold upright. Everything fell to the floor.

"What's going on?" the hero asked, trying to find the strength to lift his robotic arms.

"How can this happen? My design is flawless!" Heinsrick pulled the trigger again and again.

But it was useless. Both of their weapons had stopped working.

There was a moment of silence when no one moved, and the only sound was the vortex of a portal that was still open.

"Mecha!" A girl's voice broke the silence before she, too, came through the portal. She had blonde pigtails, was dressed in a pink suit, and held a futuristic rifle. "What did I tell you? Don't just run after him alone!"

"I don't need you lecturing me now, Ringlet!" the hero snapped back. "Call Gear, something's wrong with my arms!"

"Well, if you hadn't just run off on your own, you would've been around to hear Gear's explanation!"

"*Mecha, are you there?*" a garbled voice came over a radio. "*We don't know what kind of world you're going into. Your arms draw power from the surrounding atmosphere. If there aren't the same spiral particles in the air, then your arms aren't going to work!*"

"Mention things like that sooner!"

"Hurry up," Ringlet said, pulling him back. "We can't stay here much longer. The portal's closing."

"What about Heinsrick?"

"If he knows what's good for him, he'll follow us back."

And just like that, Mecha and Ringlet jumped back through the swirling green portal, leaving Heinsrick fiddling with his plasma guns, oblivious to the fact that the heroes had retreated.

"Eternal anguish," he muttered. "Just work already! Hey, where'd everyone go?"

Silence answered him. He looked around and his eyes met Margaret's. In a flash of panic, she looked around as if someone else had also magically appeared in her bookshop.

"They, uh…" she sputtered when no one else showed up to offer assistance. "They went back through the portal. Something about stuff not working the same here as in your world."

"You… You mean, no plasma?" The villain's face fell, and he looked like a lost child. He looked sadly at his guns, bottom lip stuck out in a pout. He quickly got over it and the scowl came back. "What a crappy world! Who needs this anyway? A world without plasma is of no use to me!"

He turned back to the portal, which seemed to be slowing in intensity, the light starting to fade away. But before he could pass through, it snapped shut. No more green glow, no swirling whirlwind. Only the book it came from.

Heinsrick stared at the open book on the counter and chuckled nervously. "Heh heh, no matter. I—I'll just create another one."

He lifted his wrist and pulled back his sleeve. Margaret felt her breath catch when she saw the Poral Generator strapped to his arm. *How did he get that? What happened to Maître? Was he alright? Wait, was that thing smoking?*

The villain started pressing buttons, but the contraption sparked, and he yanked his hand away. "Come on," he cursed as a bead of sweat formed on his brow. The shots of electricity popped each time he tried to fiddle, then all at once, a black cloud of smoke erupted from the Portal Generator, and the device broke and fell to the floor in a pile of smouldering pieces.

Both of them stared at the remains with slack jaws. Then their eyes met. It was then that Margaret remembered Maître's warning about too many people passing through the portal at once.

"It's gonna be *that* kind of day then." She sagged against the wall.

CHAPTER 5

PLASMA WAS OVERRATED ANYWAYS

"Girl," Heinsrick said, schooling his expression. She flinched. It was then that she remembered that she was still toting around the crossbow she'd found in the back. She hefted it up and pointed it at the villain. He did not look amused.

"Stop!" she said in what she hoped was a steady voice. "Just… stop."

"Come on," he rolled his eyes. "What do you think I'm gonna do?"

"Nothing good, that's for sure." Her voice cracked a little.

"And you're going to stop me with some ancient piece of wood that isn't even loaded?"

She looked at the crossbow, then to the bolt that was still in her other hand. "Oh, come on." She fought with the bow and tried to pull the string back. It moved about three inches before it cut into her fingers and snapped back. She swore and dropped the stupid thing. "Well, your weapon isn't working either!"

"It's not a relic from the stone age. Don't compare the two," he sniffed, offended.

"So… what do we do?"

"Well, I'm not sticking around in this lame world, that's for sure." He bent down and started collecting the broken pieces of the Portal Generator. "How do you even live without the benefits of plasma?"

"The what?"

"Plasma! You know, being able to disintegrate people at will, good for when you're waiting in line at the coffee shop. Then you can blast through walls and make doors wherever you want. Very convenient. Then there's the obvious: using it to destroy the world and everything on it."

"Yeah, who can live without that." She was starting to feel lightheaded.

"Duck narf! This stupid thing," he muttered, trying to smack pieces of metal together. He plopped down cross-legged on the counter. His 'plasma' guns unclipped from his arms and clattered to the floor. She flinched back at the noise and hoped to high heaven that the little twerp didn't just gouge a hole in her floor. But he was too focused on the device to notice her ire.

"What happened, anyway?" Heinsrick closed one eye and held up a piece of twisted metal. "The weirdo in the coat said this thing was foolproof."

"Weirdo? You mean Maître?"

"What kind of name is that? Naw, he didn't say who he was. He was real arrogant, though, with his stupid long coat and twisty words."

"That's him! You *stole* his Portal Generator? And *broke it*!"

"Thing broke on its own. You saw it. Useless piece of junk," he huffed and threw the pieces down in front of him. "Talk about unreliable technology. You know what never lets you down? Plasma!"

"Didn't it *just* let you down?"

"That's because your world is clearly inferior to my own."

"Getting back to the thing that *you broke*—"

"I didn't break it!"

"You did! If more than one person passes through the portal at any one time, then it starts to overload! With you and your little friends coming back and forth, it transported, like what? Five times with one portal? Just two people going one way is enough to put strain on it. Ergo, *you broke it!*"

"How was I supposed to know its limitations?" he snuffed back, then looked at her suspiciously. "How do *you* know so much about it? What exactly is your relationship with White Coat?"

"Re-relation—" She felt her face heat up. "It—it's—there's no relation-ship!" Why was she so flustered? "I just… happened to help him out one time. It was a chance encounter, that's all."

"Really?" he drawled, eyebrows raised. Her face went even redder. "Not that it matters."

She clenched her fists in irritation as he hopped off her counter and looked around her shop for the first time. "What is this place, anyway? And what's with all the books? Lame."

A vein pulsed in her forehead, and suddenly, an empty binder collided with the villain's face.

"OW! What the fraggle!" he cried out, holding his nose.

"Can you fix the stupid portal bracelet and *leave* already?" she yelled back. She couldn't wait for this twerp to be gone.

He eyed her suspiciously again. "I can try, but as I have been made aware, your world is different from my own. The technology I'm used to doesn't seem to work here."

"This isn't tech from your world," she emphasized, tapping the bracelet repeatedly. "It's not *your* tech at all. You stole it!"

"Yeah! I stole it! And it turned out to be a colossal waste of time and effort! Now, as you've pointed out, this isn't my creation, so *forgive me* if I don't immediately understand every aspect of it and can't put these itty-bitty pieces back together with magic!"

"UGH!" She threw her arms up over her face and slid down the wall in defeat. She screamed into her legs in pure frustration and pent-up stress.

The shop went quiet. She sat on the ground and Heinsrick leaned against the counter with a very confused expression on his face.

"Okay, okay," Margaret tried to talk herself through this. She rubbed at her eyes and took a deep breath. "It's okay, you're fine. It's just… things seem to have gotten a little out of hand, right? No big deal. It's only that everything you've been doubting this past week turned out to be real, and Maître can't really come back right now because some plasma obsessed brat stole his Portal Generator and broke it, and now I'm stuck with this brat until we can figure out what to do next."

"Are you done freaking out, lady?" Heinsrick interrupted.

Her eyes opened, she looked at him, then snapped them shut again. "Oh, you *are* still here."

"Was I supposed to go somewhere?"

"No, no, you're just not supposed to be real." She managed to find her feet again and stood up.

"My apologies." He rolled his eyes.

"Well, since we're down a Portal Generator, we'll just have to find the other one."

"The othe—There's another one?" He slammed his hands down on the counter. "Mention things like that sooner!"

"Bite me," she snapped back and dragged the crossbow into the back room. Heinsrick trailed after her with a scowl. He looked around the dirty room in distain. "My uncle had one a long time ago. This used to be his shop, so I'm hoping it's still around here… somewhere."

"That's all you've got to go on?" he asked, unimpressed.

"You keep flapping your mouth, and I'll find a heavier binder," she retorted. "Get to looking. And don't *break* anything."

Heinsrick grumbled as his eyes slid over the shelves of boxes and lingered on the workbench. He walked over and slid a finger over its surface, picking up a trail of dust and grime. "Gross," he commented dryly.

"So I'm not done cleaning yet—sue me. And I've already checked there."

"Have you?" he questioned, raising a taunting eyebrow.

"That's generally what 'I've already checked there' means."

"Well, by the amount of dust built up here, you haven't opened this panel yet." He jabbed a thumb toward the wall.

"What? Panel?" She came up beside him and looked at the brick wall. "There's nothing there."

"It's plain as day." He pointed to one spot that looked exactly the same as the rest of the wall.

"Clearly, all that plasma is affecting your brain."

"*Clearly*, your modulator can't even detect a hidden compartment," he shot back as he traced his finger along the wall until it caught a latch. With a cocky smirk, he flicked the hidden switch and a deep *clunk* sounded from within the wall. She watched in amazement as a square-foot section of the wall swung outward and revealed a safe that was built into the wall.

"How did you…"

"Because *my* modulator is in perfect working order." He turned and leaned against the workbench, stretching his arms behind his head.

"I don't know what a modulator is, but it seems more useful than plasma."

"Would you stop criticizing the plasma? It deserves more respect than that."

"Whatever," she mumbled and turned her attention back to the safe. Unlike everything else in the store, it was new. By new, she meant built sometime in the last decade. All it had to show was a large dial with ticks and numbers. "Now, if only we could get this open."

"You know what could get this open?"

"The combination?"

"Plasma."

"I'm going to hit you."

"Try it, doll."

Crash!

The crossbow smashed against the workbench, inches from Heinsrick's hand.

"Call me that one more time, and you'll never be able to eat again."

The look on her face made him swallow his snark. There was no anger, no sadness—heck, there wasn't even any crazy. It was just a stone cold, emotionless stare that left him feeling just a little smaller.

He nodded silently. The crossbow clattered to the floor as Margaret turned her attention back to the safe. Heinsrick eyed the ancient weapon, and tension filled his shoulders when he saw a new crack along the length of the heavy wood.

He watched her with new eyes as she played around with the safe, twisting the dial one way, then the other before trying the latch. The process repeated, and each time the rattle of the latch became more desperate as it remained locked.

"Expert safe cracker here, folks," Heinsrick couldn't help but taunt.

"You know what, you're really pushing your luck here," she said, trying to keep her fingers from shaking.

"By all means," he gestured back to the safe, "hone your skills."

"Brat," she muttered and leaned against the workbench. "The combination's gotta be around here somewhere." She started shuffling papers around.

"Yeah, because the smart thing to do with a secret combination is to write it down where thieves can find it. Seriously, you only find things like that in video games."

"Fair enough." She ran a hand over her face. "Then what do we do? We don't even know if it's in there."

"It's in there," Heinsrick said, squinting at the safe. Something flashed in his eyes. "The lead lining is blocking most of it, but I can still detect the energy it's emitting."

"How?" Her arms flopped at her side in defeat. "How can you know that?"

"Modulator, duh."

"Again, I don't know what that is!"

"You don't know?"

"No, I'm just messing with you, of course I know what it is… Idiot! This isn't your world! Whatever messed up technology and physics you had back there doesn't exist here!"

"You mean you don't have coffee machines?"

"N-no," she was taken aback. "No, we have coffee machines. I mean the more advanced stuff, like laser guns and the modu-whatevers."

"Tch, don't scare me like that," he huffed. "Well, a modulator is an extension that everyone gets."

"Extension?"

"Yeah, like an upgrade," he explained and waved her away from the safe. She watched as he started spinning the dial and caught that flash of colour in his eyes again. "A little component that gets installed once your brain has finished developing."

"Wait, wait," she held up her hands. "You mean, everyone has computer chips in their brains?"

"Crude way of putting it."

"And that works?"

"What do you mean? They wouldn't put it in if it didn't."

"No, I mean, like, no one's tried to hack into them and start mind controlling the entire population?"

He paused at that—froze, really—and he listened as she continued.

"I mean, come on, it doesn't get much more cliché than that. It's just a recipe for disaster. One hacker. That's all it takes. One hacker whose parents didn't hug him enough, or one guy spilling coffee at HQ, and suddenly the whole system fritzes out and everyone's heads start exploding!"

"Of course," he realized. "It's the perfect thing to target if you're planning on taking over the world."

"Right!" She smiled, glad someone understood. "Oh, wait, aren't you the villain of your book?"

"My what?"

"Your—" she stopped herself. Did he not know he was a character? "You know what, forget I even said anything. So, what does this moddy-thingy do?"

"Uh, it's multifunctional," he answered, put off by her reaction. "Shows a display of wherever it detects, analyses the environment, keeps track of your e-mails. Not much it can't do."

"So, a cellphone on steroids. And it can tell that the Portal Generator is in the safe?"

"And predict the combination, too." He smirked just as the safe clicked open.

"Handy," she admitted, and he stepped back with a flourish.

Inside the safe was a simple wooden box. She pulled it out and tried to blow away the thick layer of dust. She wiped away the rest, leaving her hand grimy, and placed the box on the workbench.

Heinsrick shuffled closer but stayed quiet. She paid him no mind as she hooked her fingers around the lid. It opened on stiff hinges. She half expected a synth to build up as she opened it and a bright shining light to spill out from the cracks. After all, this was the big reveal of a long-lost secret!

But there was no music, no glow. Just a sci-fi looking armband nestled in some crumpled up newspaper. It was different than the one Heinsrick had stolen. It had more ridges, more bumps. It looked older and more worn down. It was bulkier, not as elegant, and had scratches and nicks where Maître's had remained sleek and polished.

"You gonna just keep staring at it?" Heinsrick broke her from her musings.

Her eye twitched, and she glanced at where the crossbow had fallen. Instead of shooting him, she picked up her uncle's Portal Generator and turned it over in her hands until she found the clasp. Without trouble, she managed to fasten it to her own wrist.

She held it out. "How's it look?"

"Who cares?" Heinsrick grabbed her wrist and inspected it critically. "Does this piece of junk even work?"

"I don't know." She ran her fingers over the multitude of buttons and tiny dials. "How does it turn on?" She answered her own question when she pressed two buttons near the clasp. The whole thing lit up and started to whir.

"I think it works," Heinsrick grinned.

She watched in awe as pieces of the contraption started to move. Gears spun, tiny mechanisms shifted, three little bars extended over the clasp and clicked into place. More segments spun outward and revealed a screen on the face of the watch as it booted up. Pieces continued to click into place until her entire wrist and a good portion of her forearm were encased.

The awe faded, though, when she found a new problem. Her fingers fumbled over the latch, and a flash of panic shot through her. "Uh... how does it come off?"

Heinsrick stared at her for a moment, then grabbed her arm and started pulling at the Portal Generator. "You just—just pull on this... or was it this piece—OUCH!" He snatched his hand back and stuck a finger in his mouth.

"Well, how did you get it off last time?" she yelled.

"It broke off!"

"Then how did Maître take it off?"

"I don't know; it wasn't a demonstration! He took it off on his own, and I took it when he wasn't looking!"

"Why did he take it off in the first place?"

"How should I know! I don't know what that guy's thinking. All I do know is that he wanted help finding this Print thingy, and in exchange, he'd help me build something for my latest scheme. Then he mentioned how he could travel through different realities, and I just had to see it for myself. Why stop at one world when you can destroy them all!"

"But—but that doesn't make sense. Why would he help the villain?"

"I don't know. *You're* the one who's friends with the guy."

"He must have his own reasons. Maybe he just needed help finding the Print… That has to be it."

"What's so special about this Print thing anyway?"

"If I tell you, then you might want to try to destroy it."

"I *already* wanna destroy it. Now, how do you find it?"

"I don't know. He left before he finished explaining everything. Then *you* managed to trap him there."

"You're welcome. He seemed like a weirdo anyway—the kind of guy you shouldn't trust."

"Oh, and you're so much better?"

"Hey, everyone knows what I want. It's the sneaky ones you gotta look out for."

"This isn't going anywhere." She rubbed her eyes. "Can we just get going already?"

"You're coming too?"

"What, I'm supposed to trust you to give the Portal Generator back? Fat chance. Besides, I don't think this thing is coming off anytime soon." She shook her wrist for emphasis.

"Alright, fine, whatever. Tag along. But I'm not making any promises. As soon as we're back in my world, all bets are off."

"Fine by me. I'm getting sick of you anyways."

Heinsrick humphed and left the back room. She went to follow but paused when she saw the crossbow lying on the ground.

Should I bring a weapon? she wondered. She bent down to retrieve the crossbow and realized how stupid that was. She didn't even know how to shoot a crossbow. And besides, she was heading into a book where technology was advanced to the point of plasma guns and giant robotic arms. A flimsy arrow wasn't going to do much even *if* she figured out how to load it.

Then she remembered the bottom drawer of her uncle's desk and what hid inside.

She glanced toward the back of the room. A heavy stone settled in her gut. She swallowed it down and retrieved the heavy gun. She contemplated it momentarily before slipping it into the waistline of her pants. Then, making sure it was properly covered, she joined the villain, who was retrieving his own weapons that he'd brought along for the ride.

He quirked an eyebrow at her as she walked up to the counter and picked up the open book. She wondered briefly if the page it was opened to mattered. Not wanting to mess with anything, she left it open to the same page and placed it on the ground.

"What do you need that for?" Heinsrick asked, half-interested in the book.

"It's what connects the two worlds," she answered after a moment of thought.

"However *that* works." Heinsrick rolled his eyes. He really didn't know. He wasn't aware of the fact that he was just a character from a book. That his world was made up by someone else.

That's not something I'd touch with a five-foot pole, she thought grimly. She held out her arm and looked at the Portal Generator. *Just get Maître back and leave the brat back in his book. Then maybe things can go back to normal... whatever normal is at this point.*

"All right," she said aloud. "How does this thing work?"

Even as she spoke, the Portal Generator detected the open book on the floor. The screen blinked with green letters and asked her if she wanted to travel. "Easy as that, huh?" she muttered and clicked the 'Yes' button.

Loading...

Portal Initiation...

Please wait...

The face of the Generator popped up like a big button.

Launch.

"Well," she said and locked eyes with Heinsrick. "Here goes nothing."

CHAPTER 6

NEW PLACES, NEW TRAUMA

She slammed her hand down on the big button. There was a flash of green sparks, and the words on the page started glowing. Soon, they were swirling and lifting off the page. A moment later, a full swirling vortex had formed, and the wind whipped around the store.

"Finally," Heinsrick grinned. His plasma guns were strapped to his arms again. With a holler, he leapt straight into the portal and disappeared.

"My turn then." She took a deep breath and held it, caught up in the moment. Then with a shout of her own, she was flying into the portal, screaming the whole way. Wind ripped at her clothes, and her hair flew around.

Then it was quiet, and she was standing on solid ground once again. She opened one eye first, then the other.

Her jaw fell open at the world she found herself in.

Buildings, impossibly tall, loomed overhead in a cartoon-styled cityscape. Cars flew high above her in neat lines, unobstructed by traffic lights or pedestrians. She jumped back as a group of kids raced by on hoverboards, waving at her and shouting apologies before they disappeared around a corner.

She did a full three-sixty, then realized there was still a swirling green vortex behind her. "Crap!"

She fought with the Poral Generator, and after flicking through a couple of screens and pounding it with her fist, the option to deactivate the portal finally appeared. She sighed as it swirled out of existence, and traces of green letters dissolved on a passing breeze.

"So, what do we do now?" She asked breathlessly and turned to Heinsrick... who was gone. "Son of a..."

She looked around wildly, running a hand through her hair. She paused when she felt something on her head that wasn't there before. She pulled off a bulky bright yellow plastic headband that she hadn't been wearing a minute ago.

"What..."

She caught sight of herself in the reflection of a window. Her jeans and sweater were gone, replaced with a tight-fitting, plastic-looking material that was accented by more bulky accessories around her waist, shoulder, and wrists, all yellow in colour. Everyone else bustling around her was dressed similarly.

Must be part of entering fictional worlds then, she reasoned. *In order to blend in.* Her hair even looked plastic, tied up in a high ponytail with a thick, shiny elastic... if you could call it elastic because it was also hard. And the gun that she had slipped into the waistline of her pants was now gone.

"Great."

But the thought didn't stick around for long because the amazement of what was happening was starting to fade. She looked up at the impossibly tall buildings again, the flying cars, the floating platforms that hovered hundreds of feet in the air.

Now that she was here, where was she supposed to go? Heinsrick was supposed to lead her to Maître. But then again, he did say that all bets were off. So, she was alone.

Just the thought set her nerves off. Her hands turned the plastic headband over and over, and maybe, just maybe, a little moisture built up in her eyes as the panic started setting in.

She had been alone in some sense of the word for most of her life. She almost preferred it. But this was a whole new experience! She didn't know what to do. She'd never read any of the *Mecha Arms* books. The franchise gained popularity after it had been adapted into a TV show, but it was geared towards kids. She had barely recognized the heroes when they'd chased Heinsrick into the bookshop, and now she was supposed to navigate this crazy futuristic city on her own and find a man who she barely knew, who had promised to take her on adventures she couldn't even begin to imagine? And she could imagine quite a bit.

It was overwhelming, and she had to take a moment to control her breathing and maybe wipe away a tear that had managed to form.

What am I doing? I can't do this. I'm just a girl who barely has her life together. I can't just—just jump through some magical portal and become a hero!

It's not magic, Maître's voice echoed in her head. *It's science. There's a difference.*

"Who cares if there's a difference," she mumbled angrily and got a couple of weird looks for it. She ignored them and turned her attention to the Portal Generator instead.

`Warning! Portal Exertion Elevated: 35%`

Must be the more-than-one-person thing. She sighed and dropped her head against the window. *Maître, where are you?*

"Waiting for someone?"

Her head snapped up at the familiar snark, and she was *almost* relieved to see Heinsrick's cocky grin from the driver's seat of one of the flying cars.

"Took you long enough," she snapped instead, swallowing down all the panic. "I thought you'd ditched me."

"That was the plan," Heinsrick admitted, revving the engine as she took her seat beside him. "But then I remembered that you have very nice piece of technology strapped to your arm that's supposed to be mine."

"Excuse you! Yours?"

"Yes, I stole it, it's mine."

"The one you stole broke, idiot."

"And now I'm stealing you." Her heart skipped as he shifted the car into gear, and it started humming. "Now, let's get out of here before the MPF shows up."

"The what?" Her mind was reeling again.

Sirens erupted from behind, and a garbled voice started yelling over a loudspeaker. "Stop! Tidus Heinsrick, turn off the hover car and step out of the vehicle," said an authoritative voice. Her eyes widened when she saw the red and blue flashing lights, and a bunch of black and white cars slid to a stop around them.

"Local authorities," Heinsrick answered and grinned excitedly. "I *am* an evil mastermind, remember?"

She didn't have a chance to react before the hover car lurched upwards. They flew at a crazy speed, higher and higher until they broke through the first level of traffic. People swerved and honked and shook their fists as the car recklessly barreled through traffic.

Heinsrick started laughing like a madman as the MPF gave chase, their lights and sirens blaring, causing other cars to scatter even more.

"Seat belts, where are the seat belts?" Margaret fumbled along the inside of the car, looking for some sort of safety mechanism.

One police car managed to pull up alongside them, and some sort of gun rose from the roof and swiveled to point at them. Heinsrick just smirked at the danger and flicked a few switches on the dash. A gun of his own rose from the hood. The police got the first shot off. Heinsrick swerved and the blast blew a hole into a nearby building.

He laughed out the window. "Your guns are weak! Have a taste of my *plasma!*" Heinsrick's gun started glowing and fired a death ray that engulfed the entire police car, sending only a burning husk of metal crashing and falling towards the ground.

"Oh my god, oh my god, oh my god!" Margaret screamed. "You just *killed* them!"

"Relax," he said, lining up his next shot with a joystick like this was some videogame. "The MPF hover cars are controlled remotely. There's no one actually in there. Bunch of cowards."

"What about people on the street?" she screamed back. "What if it falls on them?"

"Then they shouldn't be standing there, yeesh." He smacked a few more controls and yanked the wheel down. The car responded and shot upward. Margaret sat frozen with a look of terror on her face and a death grip on the door handle. Heinsrick rolled his eyes at her. "There's a protective force field that shields the ground level from falling debris. Feel better now?"

"I'll feel better when we're on solid ground again!"

"Well, ain't that a pity." He smirked and jerked the car to the left, firing his plasma canon again. Another cop car fell. Margaret felt her stomach leave through her esophagus as the car plunged downward, all to the sound of Heinsrick's maniacal laughter.

"Look out for the—AHHH!" she screamed and shielded her face as they broke through another neat line of cars, clipping one and sending it spinning out of control as another driver panicked and rear-ended someone else. There was smoke and horns and yelling, and the sirens were persistently following them, ignoring all the chaos they were causing.

The plasma canon fired again, beaming straight through another cruiser and damaging another one behind it.

"That's a two-fer!" Heinsrick cackled.

More sirens joined the fray as backup arrived. Heinsrick narrowed his eyes and finally stopped laughing and started concentrating.

"No, no, no. Move out of the—WOAH!" Margaret kept on screaming as Heinsrick dove into the narrow spaces between skyscrapers and tried to lose the cops in a maze of streets with high speeds and narrow misses. He blasted more cop cars, clipped the sides of buildings, spun upside down, and even went into a free fall at one point.

"Would you SHUT UP!" Heinsrick screamed.

"NO, I WILL NOT!" she screamed back, then took a deep breath and kept going.

It took longer than it should have to realize that they were no longer moving. She cracked an eye open, then another, and saw that they were now stopped in the middle of the sky, well above even the tallest building. There were no cop cars, no sirens, no chase. She stole a glance at Heinsrick; the kid was watching her with an unimpressed look and hands tightly clamped over his ears.

She ignored him and looked out the window. They were high up. The city below was riddled with plumes of smoke and chaos. There were hardly any flying cars moseying around anymore except for emergency vehicles that were just starting to arrive.

"Are you done now?" the villain asked, finally unplugging his ears.

"For now," she said hoarsely, slumping down into her seat. "Can we just land already?"

"Where's your sense of fun?" he grumbled and grabbed the controls.

"It fell off somewhere during the backflip!" she snapped.

"You're still yelling!"

"And we're still flying!"

CRASH!

"Woah!" Heinsrick yanked on the wheel as something hit the car. He lost control and they started spinning through the sky.

Margaret caught a glimpse of a red car flying circles around them. Even crazier was that there was someone standing on top of it! She was pretty sure it was the kid with the robot arms from the bookshop—the hero of this story—but it was hard to tell when they were caught in a tailspin, and she was resisting the urge to start screaming again.

The gun from the red car fired again, and the shot smashed right through the front of their car. The hood flew off and the engine flared and started spewing smoke. The car careened out of control.

"Hold on!" Heinsrick yelled as he fought with the controls.

"To what?" she yelled back.

Heinsrick wrenched the wheel and managed to crash-land on the roof of the tallest building in the city. They screeched to a halt with plenty of room to spare. As soon as they came to a stop, Margaret fell out of the car, scraping her knees and gasping for air. Heinsrick followed, keeping his eyes to the sky, watching as the red car circled above.

His eyes locked onto the figure riding on the roof of the red car, and he grinned. "Mecha."

His arms snapped out and his plasma guns swiveled into place, moulding to the shape of his arms with the triggers sitting perfectly in his hand. They started whirring as they warmed up. The kid on the car jumped, breaking his fall with his robotic arms and cracking the concrete beneath him.

"What took you so long?" Heinsrick rolled his neck. "I managed to break all my toys before you even showed up."

"We weren't expecting you to show your face again so soon after your last failure," Mecha said easily.

"Just keeping you on your toes. Besides, evil doesn't take a holiday."

The air crackled with energy, and everything was still for a split second. Then, the plasma fired, and the arms flew into action. They went at each other like two hyenas fighting over the last scraps of rotten flesh.

From the sidelines, Margaret could only watch. Mecha weaved in and out of the plasma streams, maneuvering himself until he got close enough to engage in melee combat. He pushed forward with the strength of his mechanical arms, raining a torrent of blows upon Heinsrick, who defended himself using the bulk of one of his plasma guns.

But the hardware of the guns was no match. The metal bent and twisted, and fragile pieces ruptured and started to smoke. Heinsrick bounded backwards and shook off the now useless plasma gun, then fired with the other one. Mecha swiped the hunk of metal off the side of the building as he bounced out of the way.

With more distance between them, they started pacing again, circling the rooftop while exchanging banter that they probably thought was witty but was actually cringy. Margaret, on the other hand, wasn't paying too much attention. She was busy trying to make herself as small as possible and stay away from the two monster children battling it out. She was currently huddled up against the wreckage of Heinsrick's car, but a gust of wind had her looking up as the red hover car floated just a few feet away from the edge of the building.

"Hey! Are you alright?" the cute girl's voice called over the hum of the car.

Margaret pried her eyes open and saw the girl in pink with two blonde pigtails that spiraled out on either side of her. "Ringlet," she managed to remember the name of the heroine.

"Come on, I'll take you to safety!" Ringlet called encouragingly.

56

"Hell no! There is no way on God's green earth that I am *ever* getting into another one of those contraptions again! There aren't even *seatbelts!*"

The heroine's eye twitched in irritation. "Don't be stupid, just get in already!"

"No!"

"So, you'd rather stay up here while those two morons beat each other to a pulp?"

Margaret flinched and peeked over the front of the car just in time to duck out of the way as Heinsrick shot his plasma gun in her direction. Mecha lifted Heinsrick's destroyed car and threw it at the villain. A shot of plasma hit the car. It exploded into bits of shrapnel as hot liquid spewed everywhere.

Margaret curled up in a ball, expecting the sharp metal to pierce into her skin. Instead, a shadow fell over her as Mecha brushed the shrapnel out of the air with his arms, shielding her from harm. Then, the hero was off again, crossing the roof and leaving her to make her choice.

"Fine!" Margaret conceded and stubbornly crawled on shaky legs towards the edge of the roof.

"We don't have all day," Ringlet said, impatiently tapping the wheel.

"Shut it!"

Margaret managed to get her unsteady legs underneath her to support some fraction of her weight.

Ringlet pulled the hover car closer to the building, and the back door swung open. Margaret leaned against the short stone wall that surrounded the edge of the roof and made the mistake of looking down… and down and down, all the way to the very hard ground that was very far away.

"Ha ha ha!" A goofy smile born of pure panic spread across her face. "Nope." She shook her head and sunk to the ground again, huddled against the short wall as her entire body started trembling. She curled even further into herself as another blast set off some sort of explosion. "Nope, nope, nope. Just a big ol' bag of nopedy-nope-nope."

"Come *on*," Ringlet yelled, desperation starting to seep into her voice.

Another blast of plasma shot toward the red car, and Ringlet slammed into gear and zoomed upward just before it hit. Heinsrick was suddenly right there with his back to her.

"You're not going anywhere with that thing on your wrist," the villain said while keeping his attention on his opponent.

She looked up at him. He was more than just a kid with wild hair and crazy sci-fi plasma guns that had the potential to level an entire city. He was more than just a brat. He was confident in his abilities. His plans always failed but he managed to effortlessly get back up even though all his hard work had just been thoroughly stomped on and destroyed.

She used a page out of Heinsrick's book. She took a deep breath, and even though the wind was blowing hard, the building was crumbling from the intense battle, and every single one of her limbs was shaking uncontrollably, she rose to her feet.

"The only place I'm going is wherever Maître is," she said. At least, it was what she was trying to say. It ended up sounding more like a series of squeaks, and the words that *were* comprehensible were drowned out by another barrage from Mecha. Heinsrick pushed her away from the fight and met Mecha midway with full force.

Margaret fell down... and down...

Arms crashed against reinforced steel as their weapons locked together and the boys grappled for control.

"What's your plan this time?" Mecha asked between clenched teeth. "First you try teleporting through dimensions, and now you're kidnapping civilians?"

"Trust me, she's not all she's cracked up to be," Heinsrick snarked.

Mecha scrunched his face in concentration and pushed forward again, but the unstable ground had him losing his footing. Heinsrick took the opening and triggered a mechanism from his belt. A dozen small metal balls shot out and started circling in the air. Their seams glowed a deadly red. A string of energy snapped between them, connecting them in a cage of red plasma around the fallen hero.

"No!" Mecha shouted and pounded his arms against the force field.

"Gets 'em every time." Heinsrick patted himself on the back.

A distant *pop!* Sounded, and one of the metal balls was shot down.

"Forgetting someone?" Ringlet's voice swept over the rooftop. The front windshield of the red hover car had been retracted, and she took aim with her rifle as she lined up her next shot.

Pop! Pop! Pop!

One by one, the metal balls were shot down, and the forcefield cage disintegrated.

"No!" Heinsrick cursed.

"One hundred percent charged," Mecha grinned, and his arms started glowing brightly.

"Should've seen this one coming." Heinsrick backed up, looking over his shoulder for Margaret. "Alright girly, time to—" She was gone. "Come on!"

Margaret was currently watching from the backseat of Ringlet's car, right where the heroine had caught her after Heinsrick basically pushed her off the building! To say her nerves were shot was an understatement. She was basically catatonic, too afraid to even move in case a slight shift in weight caused the car to crash and burn.

"Heaven's—" Mecha chanted. He braced his legs as the energy pooled in the palms of his robotic arms. "—Punch!"

"Plasma Shield!" Heinsrick pulled up in a last-ditch effort.

The energy focussed into a beam as Mecha punched at the air, triggering the Spiro Particles resonation effect. The resulting blast ripped through Heinsrick's improvised shield and blew apart the rest of the roof along with the top three stories of the building.

Margaret recoiled from the window as the blast rocked the car, and Ringlet rose out of the blast radius. The light faded, and what was left of the roof crumbled. The destruction was absolute except for a small circle where Mecha stood untouched.

It was quiet as Ringlet pulled up alongside him, and the hero jumped onto the roof of the car. Something mechanical whirred as parts of the car secured Mecha's arms in place before he was released from the heavy burden and slipped into the passenger seat.

Margaret pressed her forehead against the window, eyes searching the wreckage, but Tidus Heinsrick was nowhere to be seen.

CHAPTER 7

ARCADES CAN STILL BE COOL

S he didn't know where they were going, but for some reason, she couldn't find the energy to care. All the adrenaline was finally wearing off, and her mind was in turmoil after everything that had happened.

They said he couldn't have died and that he's survived worse. If it was that easy to kill Tidus Heinsrick, the city wouldn't need heroes. It didn't reassure her.

After the explosion, Margaret had snapped out of her reverie. But just because she wasn't catatonic anymore didn't mean she wasn't still a panicked wreck. And now she was with people she didn't know, and her brain was screaming *'Stranger Danger!'* even though she was significantly older than them.

Her current situation was just the icing on the cake of traumatizing events. She had half a mind to just call it quits, figure out how to open the portal, and go back to the real world where her biggest problem was making sure the shop was ready for opening day. She still had to finish going through all her stock, organizing everything, last minute clean up, and maybe even go through the junk in the back room...

Her tense muscles started to loosen as her mind thought about the more menial tasks of everyday life. From the front seat, Mecha and Ringlet exchanged looks.

Margaret stared at her knees, lost in thought as the hover car flew away from all the wreckage and chaos, and they merged into the evening traffic, indistinguishable from the rest of the cars. They drove through the airborne streets, descending until they reached ground level and floated along the asphalt roads. It wasn't much longer until they pulled into a parking lot and the engine shut off.

She finally looked up when she heard her door open, and Ringlet offered a hand to help her out. Both Ringlet and Mecha were now in civilian clothes that were similar to the jumpsuit Margaret had. She hesitantly took the outstretched hand and stepped out into the cool evening air. She looked around, seeing none of the earlier chaos surrounding them. They were now on a calm street with groups of kids playing and teenagers hanging out in circles or riding hoverboards. A few were even racing drones.

She followed Ringlet to a one-story building, dwarfed by all the high-rises and megamalls that surrounded it. The building was marked with bright LED letters above the front doors that read 'ARCADE.' The letters faded between colours and cast a glow around the parking lot.

Mecha took the lead and pushed the doors open. Margaret was hit by a wall of noise from excited kids and arcade games and the smell of sweat, candy, and greasy food thrown into the mix for good measure.

Row after row of colourful arcade games filled the large room, from shoot 'em ups to racing, basketball, and even VR experiences. Kids were scattered around the place, absorbed in the games and competitions or just hanging out with friends and sharing pizza.

Mecha waved to the guy manning the front desk, which also doubled as the prize counter. The guy nodded back and pressed a button under the counter, unlocking a door near the back of the arcade that was nestled between Zombie Hunters VIII and Mr. Dot Eater. A metal plaque on the door told kids 'DO NOT ENTER' and just begged mischievous children to try their luck. Mecha held the door open and ushered everyone through.

The noise dissolved into nothing as they left the arcade behind. Margaret no longer had the energy to be surprised to find herself in the heroes' secret hideout. One half was a mess of parts, tools, and equipment, topped off with a messy workstation and a wall of computer monitors. It was an engineer's dream. The other half was a lot more organized with a long conference table and a white board. The small kitchenette seemed out of place, but it led to a short hallway that led to more rooms.

Inside the mechanical part of the room, a computer chair swiveled away from the numerous monitors. A teenager in a black suit with messy dark hair, thin glasses, and a headset examined her critically. "Since when do we show random strangers our secret base?"

"Since she needs help," Ringlet shot back. "This is Gear. He's the smarts behind our operation. The guy working the front counter of the arcade is his cousin, Ray. He owns this place and lets us use the back room as our HQ."

"Still don't get why you brought her *here*," Gear sighed and dumped himself into one of the chairs around the conference table.

"Where else are we going to bring her? She needs our help!"

"With what? Revealing our location to the enemy?"

"She's not helping him!" Ringlet insisted. "He was threatening her!"

"Gear's right," Mecha broke in, sliding into the seat beside the young genius. "We don't know who she is and revealing our base was a risk." Gear shot a triumphant smile at Ringlet, who glared back. "That being said," Mecha continued, "we couldn't exactly just leave her on her own. We may not know how, but she's wrapped up in this one way or another. What we need now is an explanation, not an argument."

It was Ringlet's turn to look smug while Gear rolled his eyes.

Margaret still stood awkwardly by the door. She wasn't sure what to do or say. She didn't know these people, and even though they were younger and over a head shorter than her, she couldn't help but feel intimidated by what she'd seen so far.

When Ringlet waved her over to the table, she sat on the edge of a chair and interlocked her hands in her lap. She glanced around at them, waiting for them to say something. When no one else started, Gear sighed loudly.

"Let's just get this over with. Are you helping Heinsrick or not?"

She flinched at his harsh words.

"Gear!" Ringlet scolded.

"Classy," Mecha rolled his eyes.

"Figured we should just cut straight to the point," Gear shrugged.

"Um…" Margaret shrank back into her chair. She didn't know how to answer.

"Just give it a break," Mecha cut in and turned to Margaret. "Sorry, everyone's been kind of on edge lately."

"Yeah," Ringlet jumped in. "Heinsrick's been up to something. Ever since he joined up with White Coat."

Margaret felt her stomach drop. "Who?"

"Someone new," Mecha answered ominously. "Don't know much about him, just that he came out of nowhere and teamed up with Heinsrick. He's helping him build something that will let him teleport between dimensions. Scary thing is it works. But our weapons don't seem to work properly in this other dimension, so hopefully that'll set their plans back and buy us some time."

"You mean he actually wants to take over other worlds?" Margaret asked incredulously.

"What else would an evil mastermind do with a portal to infinite dimensions?"

"I don't know. He didn't seem very interested in it after learning that he couldn't use his precious plasma," she muttered and slumped back in her seat.

"So, you *do* know something!" Gear bit at her.

"Back off, Gear," Ringlet growled.

"Why can't you see that she's obviously in league with him?"

"Because it's obvious that she *isn't!*"

"Okay, okay!" Mecha mediated. "Pipe down, both of you. Instead of arguing, why not just ask her?"

"Already tried that," Gear muttered.

Their eyes all fell to Margaret. She wasn't sure how to answer. Should she tell them everything? Would they assume she's a bad guy when she told them she was looking for Maître? Then again, why had Maître teamed up with this book's villain in the first place? He was trying to find the book's Print… but to team up with Tidus Heinsrick? He hardly seemed like the type to tolerate the loud and obnoxious teenager. Her mind was a jumble.

She didn't know what to think. But she wouldn't know anything for sure until they met up again. She decided not to think about it for now.

But the heroes were still expecting her to say something. So, she answered as best she could. "I'm not in league with Heinsrick," she said slowly.

"Told you!" Ringlet stuck her tongue out.

"Doesn't explain why she was with him," Gear countered.

"He's after this," Margaret held up her wrist and showed off the Portal Generator. She shouldn't go too far into detail about the watch. She wasn't about to drop the bomb and tell them that they were in a fictional world. She still had to be careful.

"Is that…" Gear breathed and grabbed her wrist for a closer look.

"It's a Portal Generator," Margaret explained. "It's like the one that Heinsrick got a hold of. The portal that he opened—the portal you two chased him through—it led to *my world*. Into my shop."

The kids' faces turned up in surprise. She continued.

"So many people passing through the portal at once created a sort of strain on the device, and as soon as you two left, the Portal Generator that Heinsrick had stolen broke, and the portal closed before he could go back."

"Then how is he here now? And why did you come along?" Mecha asked.

"Just so happened that my late uncle wasn't a stranger to hopping between dimensions. He had his *own* Portal Generator hidden in the shop. But as soon as I put it on, it locked onto my arm and won't come off."

"Wait." Gear waved his hands. "So, hopping through dimensions is common enough in your world that you can just *have* one of these things laying around?"

"Er… not quite. It's complicated."

"And the reason you tagged along?" Mecha asked again.

Why *had* she come? To make sure that Maître hadn't gotten himself stranded in a foreign world with no way out? Should she tell them that?

"Isn't it because Heinsrick wanted the technology for himself?" Ringlet answered for her. "He broke his, so he needs a new one. And since it's stuck to her, well…"

"Hmm," Gear twisted Margaret's arm this way and that to examine the intricate mechanisms with the critical eye of an engineer. He took note of the craftsmanship and design, tried moving the plates that locked the device to her, then started playing with the interface.

The conversation restarted around him as he tinkered.

"So, if you have this thing, why not just go back?" Mecha asked.

"Huh?"

"Can't you just open another portal and go back home?"

"I guess I could."

Gear glanced up at her suspiciously. "Unless there's some other reason why you can't."

Here it was, the '*Aw, screw it*' moment.

"I'm looking for someone," she admitted. "About a week ago, my... friend came here. He said there was something he had to take care of and that he'd be back soon. I got excited when I heard the portal open again, but..."

"Instead you got us," Ringlet finished.

"Yeah. The Portal Generator Heinsrick had was my friend's. He stole it. So, I came to make sure he had a way back... so he wouldn't be trapped here."

"A week ago, you said," Mecha thought. "Isn't that around the time White Coat showed up?"

"Now that you mention it," Ringlet tilted her head, "it would make sense if he was from another world."

"Uh, yeah," Margaret couldn't meet their eyes. "From what you guys are saying, I'm pretty sure this White Coat guy may be who I'm looking for."

"I knew it!" Gear jumped up and slammed his hands on the table.

"But it doesn't make sense." Margaret shook her head. "There has to be something I'm missing. He wouldn't just help the bad guy. Especially one as annoying as *him*."

"Where are you going with this?" Mecha asked, more cautious now than he was before.

"I—" she stuttered. "I don't know. Maybe there's something else going on, something we don't know. He wants to do *research*, not take over worlds."

"Oh, please," Gear crossed his arms and glared.

"I mean—"

"Of course, it's *possible*," Ringlet shoved Gear aside and took the seat beside Margaret. "It's not like we've ever actually caught a glimpse of White Coat. All we know is what Heinsrick has gloated about: that White Coat is helping him build something."

"Like another Portal Generator?" Margaret asked.

"Could be."

"Or it could be something more deadly," Gear muttered. "Something that'll blow up the entire city!"

"Enough!" Mecha announced. The two stopped bickering and turned to their leader. "All right then."

"All right?" Gear asked, fearing the tone in the hero's voice.

"We'll help you find your friend," Mecha nodded.

"Really?" Gear slammed his face onto the table.

"Of course, that's what we do. We help people."

"We stop crazy people from blowing things up," Gear clarified.

"*Which* is the same as helping people." Mecha smiled at his own logic.

"This isn't like looking for a lost cat."

"We're not looking for a cat, silly," Ringlet teased. "A person is much easier to spot."

"You too?"

Ringlet smiled innocently.

"Fine!" Gear threw his hands up. "You guys go looking for your lost friend who's probably busy making some death ray that'll blow us all to little bits."

"Big on the blowing up of things today, aren't you?" Mecha nudged him.

"*Meanwhile*," Gear pushed him and stalked away, "I'll be here, being *reasonable*, fixing whatever you managed to break this time." He shook his head and let the door shut behind him as he went to retrieve the arms still latched to the car out back.

Margaret watched him leave, and the anxiety started creeping up.

"Don't mind Gear," Ringlet assured her. "He's just worried. He doesn't like staying behind the scenes. He wishes he could be out there fighting with us sometimes."

"He seems like a smart guy," Margaret said. "Couldn't he just build something to fight with?"

"He's always building stuff. He's good at that. But not so much when it comes to using them."

"Hm," she acknowledged the words and stared at the door the boy had disappeared through.

A moment later, a rumbling pulled her from her troubles, and a portion of the wall started rising. She realized it was a garage door. Gear backed the red hover car into the lair, right into his workshop.

Mecha helped him unhook the two long black boxes on the roof that his arms had compacted into so that they blended in with ordinary traffic.

As the boys worked on their toys, Ringlet brought Margaret a cup of cocoa.

■—■—■—■ ▢ ■—■—■—■

Deep within the villain's lair, a heavy metal door whooshed open, and a singed and half beaten Tidus Heinsrick stomped in. His agitation was through the roof. He dumped his plasma cannons onto a workbench and continued stomping around his lair.

"I take it your little outing didn't go as planned," a suave voice echoed around the metal walls.

"Eat a bag," Heinsrick growled at the man in the white coat, who was busy tinkering with his own things.

"That's what happens when you mess with things that you don't understand," White Coat responded, not bothering to turn around to face the child. "I'll have it back now," he beckoned, sticking an open hand out behind him.

"Your dumb watch broke." Heinsrick crossed his arms, not in the least bit sorry. "Thing was barely functional. Piece of junk."

The man in the white coat sighed and removed his safety goggles. "Of course, you managed to break it. What did you do? Throw it off a cliff?"

"Please," Heinsrick scoffed. "It literally fell apart."

"After which you decided to go on a rampage throughout the city?" White Coat gestured to the large screen that was tuned in to the news channel. Cameras panned over the destruction that had been brought about that day.

"Hey, they started chasing *me*."

"Because you're a criminal."

"You aren't so good yourself, buddy."

"Good and bad are societal constructs that change depending on culture, population, and whoever seems to be in charge."

"Oh yeah, pull out your big words. Weirdo."

"Such a child." White Coat sighed and put down what he was working on. He turned to face Heinsrick with a look of annoyance.

"Just finish your work and you're free to go," Heinsrick growled. He flicked his wild hair and made his way deeper into the facility. A small robotic drone followed behind him, chattering about the city's goings on and damage reports, which the young villain found overly entertaining.

The man in the white coat shook his head as the boy genius walked off his most recent defeat. He was starting to get sick of the impudent child. But no matter, he should be done using these facilities by morning. Then, all he had to do was return to fetch his new assistant, and he could *finally* return to his work. And things would be going much smoother now that Kenneth was out of the picture—the old fool.

He stopped. The name bounced around in his head.

They had been enemies, yes, but it had been... almost fun, in a sense. He supposed it was much like what young Heinsrick and *his* nemesis had going on, just not so devastating. Or had it been?

Either way, the new Portal Generator was almost done. He'd been planning these new upgrades ever since he'd been trapped in that book. He just had one more thing to finish before he tested it out.

Then the real fun was going to begin.

The 'DO NOT ENTER' door closed gently behind Margaret as she entered the arcade once again. The young heroes had decided to have a strategy meeting, and it had seemed like a private affair, so she'd taken the hint. She just hoped that whatever they were discussing wasn't whether or not they actually trusted her.

She leaned against the wall and let the atmosphere of the arcade surround her. The cacophony of the games' music mixed with the chatter and cheers of kids playing had her reminiscing about the afternoons when her brother would drag her away from her big comfy chair and her many books. Together, they would leave the house, because mother wouldn't let them go out alone, and they would ride the bus to the only true remaining arcade in their home city. Her brother would run wild, cracking high scores and racking up tickets while she sat by the food counter and dove back into her book.

It was comforting to know that the environment was the same even in a fictional world. It was with a fond smile that she found herself sliding onto a bar stool by the food counter, wishing she had a book, but soaking up the atmosphere and trying, for just a moment, to forget the mess and chaos that had recently encroached on her life.

"Can I get you something?" a man asked from behind the counter.

She opened her eyes and looked up at a guy with curly hair as he wiped his hands on a cloth and looked at her curiously. He couldn't have been much older than herself.

"You're… Gear's cousin?"

"Name's Ray." He smiled and extended a hand over the counter.

"Margaret." She shook his hand.

"So," he drummed his fingers on the counter between them, "get you something?"

She sighed and rubbed her eyes, suddenly feeling *very* tired, which honestly wasn't surprising after everything that had happened. "You got any hard liquor?"

"Let's see." He turned to the soda fountain and squinted in concentration. "I can do a mean rum and coke, minus the rum."

"Probably as good as I'm gonna get." She leaned her elbows against the counter.

He smiled again and filled a tall glass, topping it off with a candy-striped straw and sliding it over to her. She took a sip and pretended that the cool beverage took off some of the edge. "Hits the spot."

"So," Ray folded his arms across his chest and leaned against one hip, "you've managed to get into the team's inner circle. Congrats."

69

"You make it sound like something I should be excited about."

"Most kids in this city would be thrilled to have a chance to meet *the* Mecha Arms."

"Oh, *the* Mecha Arms, is it?"

"You know—saves the city, defeats the bad guy? Typical childhood aspirations."

"And everyone's okay with a child fighting their battles for them?"

"Well, there's only so much the MPF can do."

She sighed and flicked her straw. "Why are cops always so useless in stories?"

"They do their best, I guess. Although nowadays, it's more like they're only acting as support for the Team rather than actually helping."

She cocked an eyebrow at him to emphasize her point, and he raised his hands in defence. "Okay, you got a point there. But you still haven't answered my question."

"What was the question again?"

"How did you manage to get involved in all this?"

"Oh, that question." She drew patterns in the water drops on the glass. "They haven't told you anything?"

"I pick up bits here and there. But you just popped up out of nowhere."

"Literally." she rolled her eyes. He leaned closer in interest. "To make a long story short, I got sucked into a portal and ended up in a... well, I guess this is another world? Another dimension? Whatever you want to call it." *Technically true.* She'd stick with it for now.

Ray's eyebrows shot up. "So, you're literally out of this world."

She stared at him blankly. "That was so bad it's not even funny."

"Sorry," he chuckled at himself.

"Instead of crummy pick-up lines, why not tell a girl about this world?"

"I take it that it's different from yours?"

"Technologically, I'd say you're like a full century ahead of us. And not everyone wears matching jumpsuits. There's a little more variety. But why don't we start with the kids that seem to save the world on a regular basis?"

Ray grinned and rubbed his hands together. "Alright, I've been practicing this one." He clapped, and she smiled at his enthusiasm. "Well, first off, you've got Mecha Arms himself. The hero in red. He wields level seven robotic arms, is certified by the MPF, and is acknowledged by the Lead Government as a last line of defence. But behind the arms, he's just a regular kid."

She applauded his dramatics, and he took it as his cue to continue. "Next up is Ringlet, the cutie in pink. Rational and caring, always pulling Mecha out of a tight pinch. She's the best backup a guy can ask for. The reason behind his brawn."

Ray was on a role and went right to his finale. "Finally, the man behind the scenes lending support from the shadows, and the one who personally built the arms from the ground up, Gear. Certified genius. He may have a bit of a temper, but once you get to know him, you'll find his loyalty knows no end."

"You should be an announcer," she chuckled as he took a bow.

"One of these days, my talents will be acknowledged," he sighed wistfully.

"Alright," she said. "So, a team of overpowered pre-teens saving the world... from what?"

"Anyone and everything," his eyes sparkled again. "From natural disasters to evil overlords, they keep the peace and send the bad guys packing."

"Bad guys? As in, there's more than just Heinsrick?"

"There have been others, but he's their arch-enemy *and* the biggest threat." Ray paused, and his thoughts seemed to overtake him. He became serious. "And this most recent scheme he's cooking up seems different from the others."

"Oh yeah?"

"Something's not right about it." His serious tone melted away. "Just a bad feeling. What do I know?" His smile tried to hide his concerns, but Margaret could see his eyes dim.

She hummed and shifted in her seat. A change in subject seemed best. "What about these other villains that have plagued this city? What were they like?"

He leaned against the counter and pondered. "There've been so many, it's hard to keep track of them all." His dramatics had faded. He must not have practiced this one. She smiled. "There was this one guy who didn't like how far the city was expanding and engineered these plants that could grow really fast. He tried to overgrow the whole city. There was a group of ninjas who had a beef with the International Bank's manager and held all the branches hostage. There've been a few elemental-type fighters who just wanted to test themselves but still caused quite the ruckus."

"I don't know why I expected anything better."

"Then there are things like natural disasters, tsunamis, earthquakes—you know, there was a threat of a volcano at some point."

"A volcano?"

"Didn't even know there was one around here. Oh! And aliens. There *have* been aliens."

"Huh. Never a dull moment."

"Something always seems to be going on." Ray frowned at the thought. "But what about your dimension? What's crime fighting like there?"

"Don't get me wrong, we've got problems, too. Wars, cults, terrorists. But most of the stuff closer to home is like breaking and entering, drunk driving, drugs, murder. Low key stuff."

"Murder is low key?"

"As opposed to aliens and volcanoes? Yes. Yes, kind of low key."

"Well, at least the world is still messed up, even across the multiverse. Good to know it's consistent."

"Small victories," she muttered and slurped the rest of her coke like it was hard whisky.

"Ma'am? Ma'am, I'm sorry, but I'm gonna have to cut you off." He took the empty glass from her hands.

"Jerk."

"Alright, then. How about we talk about something a little less depressing."

"Like what?"

"Tell me about yourself," he said simply. She looked up at him and found his stare intense and serious. "What led you down this path? Why are you really here?"

She stared back, thinking she saw something about this guy that drew her to him. She almost wanted to tell him about all the chaos that led her to where she was now, even before she inherited the shop, but that wasn't exactly 'less depressing.'

Even now, thinking about it brough down the mood.

The betrayal.

It sounded dramatic when put like that, but that's what it was.

She had a group of friends in college, people she'd known for years. They hung out, studied together, made memories… but apparently their bond wasn't as strong as she'd thought.

She knew that Professor Stuart's class was hard and had a low average. It was a class meant to weed out students. But instead of studying harder, they decided to take the easy way out.

A close call and a police search later, test answers were found in her backpack, stashed there by her so-called friends. She pleaded her case, tried to explain she had no part in it. She tried to explain how there was no way her friends would do something as stupid as stealing test answers.

She was wrong about that.

They threw her under the bus.

Margaret was expelled. Her college career was cut short and her life, everything she'd been working up to, was gone. She had nothing left—no goals to work towards, no friends or trust to give…

Then, her uncle's letter came, and with it, a little hope.

A new start.

Instead of blurting all of this out to a literal stranger, she broke eye contact and spun on the bar stool to look out at the rows of arcade games.

"Sorry, you'll need that rum to unlock the tragic backstory."

CHAPTER 8

WHEN IN DOUBT, BLOW IT UP

"What are these?" Margaret asked, peering into the small paper bag Ray had placed in front of her.

"Tokens," he smiled. "Figured you might get bored of just talking to this goof. And if you're looking for a challenge—you know, not to brag or anything—but I'm a god when it comes to Robo-Slayer: Redemption."

"Perks of owning an arcade." She jangled the bag.

The atmosphere had grown lighter as the conversation veered to more mundane things. She smiled and played along with his seemingly random topics, and the conversation flowed easily. She usually wasn't the type for small talk and chatting, but it wasn't long before she realized that she enjoyed Ray's company. He was a very likeable character.

But that's all he was…

A character.

In a young readers' superhero book.

Nothing new, I guess. Just another fictional boy to add to the list.

Even so, he was right in front of her. *Right there.* How could this not be real? Was it real? Wasn't this entire place just a fabrication? A couple of words strung into sentences to fill some pages in a book?

Ray looked at her expectantly, waiting for a response to his challenge.

"You're on." She grinned and swiped the paper bag of tokens off the counter.

Something flickered out of the corner of her eye. One of the game's screens started to fuzz. Then, all the screens in the arcade started flickering.

"I don't like the look of that," Ray frowned.

Some of the gamers started protesting and smacking the machines in hopes that a little violence would get the game going again. Ray didn't bother trying to stop them. He grabbed a remote and tried flicking through the channels of the TV behind the counter.

Nothing. Just static.

"Here's that bad feeling I mentioned," Ray muttered under his breath.

"What's—"

All the screens snapped into focus. A familiar face blinded them. She groaned and covered her face in exasperation as Tidus Heinsrick cackled through every speaker in the arcade.

"Head me citizens!" the villain's voice boomed. Someone booed, and the kids started buzzing.

"Not again."

"Didn't he destroy half of the downtown area already today?"

"This time! I have risen to the peak of my power!" Heinsrick swept his arm back, and the camera panned to what lay behind him. "Behold, the Shell of Vengeance!"

He was on top of another high-rise with only the sky as his backdrop. There was a machine the size of a barrel that was full of wires, flashing lights, and metal beams all circling out from an impressive-looking control panel with a very cliché-looking timer that was set for twelve hours.

But it wasn't the villain or the death machine that had her knocking her stool over and slamming her hands on the counter. Leaning right up against the Shell of Vengeance was a man with a dark ponytail and a long white coat that danced in the wind.

She would have missed Heinsrick's next words if he hadn't shoved his face in front of the camera again.

"Thanks to my new assistant, I have gained the power of interdimensional travel!" he announced.

"Then get lost!"

"In celebration of this achievement," Heinsrick's smile spread wide in a way that could only be described as evil, "I've decided to blow up the half of the city that I didn't destroy earlier! Hope you're feeling up to it, Mecha, 'cause this one's gonna be big! You have twelve hours to find me. Good luck."

The evil cackling stuttered as the feed flickered again right before all the screens snapped off. The arcade was silent for a whole second before excited chatter exploded for the coming battle. People speculated about where Heinsrick had set up this time, which set of arms Mecha would bring, what was with this new guy and, the biggest question, *interdimensional travel?*

Margaret didn't hear any of it. She slumped against the counter. "You sure you don't have any liquor?"

■—■—■—■□■—■—■—■

"I told you!" Gear slumped back in his swivel chair. "Her so-called *friend* is in league with the enemy!"

"We don't know that for sure," Ringlet tried, wanting desperately to believe.

"No," Mecha said, siding with Gear. "I think it's pretty clear which side White Coat is on. But that doesn't mean Margaret's in on it too."

Gear narrowed his eyes but didn't comment.

Ringlet twisted a lock of blonde hair around her finger. "So, what do we do?"

"We do what we always do." Mecha smiled at her. "We find the bad guy and kick him sky high."

"And the chick?" Gear pointed out. He brought up the live security footage from the arcade where Margaret was sitting at the food counter talking with Ray.

"She stays here," Mecha insisted. "You'll have to watch after her, Gear."

"What?" His chair spun to face Mecha.

"It's too dangerous for her to go out looking for White Coat if he's going to turn on her."

"And what if she turns on *us*?"

"All the better to keep an eye on her then," Mecha said, meeting Gear's glare. "Either way, she's staying. How are the arms coming?"

Gear growled and turned back to his workbench. "I'm still working on the patch job. With so little time, I can only get them operating at full power for an hour. If you go down to fifty percent, you triple your time."

"Only an hour?"

"Give me a break; this isn't simple rocket science. This is delicate machinery, man. And I usually don't have to work under pressure."

"All right, all right." Mecha waved his arms to placate the mechanic.

"We have twelve hours," Ringlet said. "That's more time than he usually gives us, so let's use it. While Mecha and I are looking for the bomb, Gear can patch up the arms as best he can."

"I'll have 'em ready for the final showdown." Gear hoisted a wrench onto his shoulder and moved to where some spare parts and pieces were all spread out. Different sets of mechanical arms hung from the wall. Gear tapped one with his wrench and turned to Mecha. "In the meantime, take a spare set. They're not outfitted to stand up to Heinsrick's Helix Plasma, but they'll tide you over."

"Right," Mecha nodded.

■–■–■–■▢■–■–■–■

Margaret sat frozen at the food counter. The news anchor on TV rattled off updates of Heinsrick's latest threat. The arcade was quiet. Everyone had been sent home to reinforced apartments or local shelters built to withstand nuclear strikes in light of the super villains that regularly plagued the city.

It was disconcerting. The once lively place filled with colours, music, and laughter now echoed with the news woman's voice. She kept repeating the same things over and over again. Take shelter, stay tuned, and wait for the heroes to save the day.

Margaret had stopped listening long ago. Conflicting thoughts tormented her frazzled mind. She saw an image of a white coated man leaning casually against a weapon of mass destruction every time she closed her eyes.

He had seemed so at ease, like he belonged there. It didn't look like he was being *forced* into building weapons. *Is… is Maître really siding with the villain here?*

She slumped and ran her hands through her hair. The yellow plastic headband clattered onto the counter. She'd forgotten she was wearing it. The hair accessory had appeared along with her jumpsuit when she entered this world, just like magic.

It wasn't hers. It didn't belong to her. It belonged to the world she was in.

Her turmoil melted away and was replaced once again by wonder as it all came rushing back to her again. She was really *inside a book*! With a shaking breath, she wandered to the front of the arcade and pressed her forehead against the tinted window. She looked up at the city from the ground and marveled at it all.

Buildings made entirely of glass shot through the sky. Floating elevators housed sports arenas and parks. Holographic advertising screens were made of nothing but light. All these impossible things had been brought to life by the magic of *words*. Only this time, it wasn't just a movie playing in her head. It was *real*! Children had *actually* flown by her on hoverboards. People passed by her on the street. Characters fought in epic battles on rooftops at impossible heights!

This was *real*. Books were so much more than just the author's imagination. They literally created worlds, people, technology, *everything*. And they didn't even know it…

She couldn't describe how she felt in that moment.

But she did know one thing.

If it wasn't for him, I'd still be sitting back at the shop. He brought me here, kind of…

Margaret had come to a new city for a new start, a new adventure, and she'd found so much more. This was just the beginning.

She stepped out onto the deserted streets. Everything lit up in a myriad of colourful lights as the sun dipped behind skyscrapers. The wind whipped between the buildings and yanked at her hair. She wrestled with it before turning into the gale.

This was her first trial—her first ordeal to overcome. She had let Tidus Heinsrick back through the portal in order to find Maître again. She knew he was here now, in this book. Sure, he may be with the villain, but come on! She'd read countless books centered around the villain. And as far as villains go, Heinsrick wasn't *all* that bad. He was likable enough from a character standpoint. He was a little crazy with his witty banter and plasma. Quirky, but not terrible.

So, Maître teamed up with Heinsrick. So, he built a bomb meant to destroy the city... Okay, maybe it wasn't so great, but she'd ask about his reasoning once they were together again.

Her objective hadn't changed. She needed to meet up with Maître, and staying here wasn't going to help with that. She doubted Mecha and the team would be willing to help. With that broadcast, they'd be convinced Maître was the bad guy; there was really no way around that. They probably wouldn't trust *her* either.

"Guess that Gear kid was right after all," she muttered as the wind died down and her hair settled into a messy tangle.

"So, you're going to go find him?"

She spun at the sound of Ray's voice. The arcade doors closed behind him. He had thrown on a dark grey jacket over his striped uniform shirt. His eyes looked sad and knowing as if he knew what she was planning.

She didn't know what to say. In the short time since she'd met him, she'd come to like this fictional character. If they were in the real world, she imagined she would have given him her phone number. She didn't like the thought of disappointing him.

"I—" Her words failed.

"It's okay," he said softly. His smile was small and melancholy. "You're not from this world. You don't belong here."

The harsh words shot through her heart, and she suddenly couldn't meet his gaze. "Don't worry," her voice was small, "I'll be out of your hair soon enough."

Ray shook his head, dark curls bouncing. "That's not what I meant. It's as if you're disturbing the very essence of this world. You're not supposed to be here."

Her eyes snapped back up to him. She considered his words. It made sense that the storyline would be thrown off by an extra character. "How can you tell? Is it those brain chips?"

His eyes lost focus as if he was seeing something far away. "Call it intuition," he said. "I've always been in touch with the underlying nature of things. I'm still not sure what to make of it myself."

"Sounds like there's more to you than just a guy behind the prize counter," she joked with a strained smile.

"Could say the same about you." The seriousness was gone from his expression and replaced by that soft smile. Her heart twitched. The wind picked up again. "Heinsrick's main base of operation is about an hour's drive by hover car, near the outskirts of the city."

"Huh?"

"You want to find your white-coated friend, right?" Ray asked.

"Well—"

"Chances are that he's holed up there."

"Why are you telling me this? Don't you think I'll team up with them?"

"Are you planning to?"

She fidgeted and shrugged.

"Margaret," he said, "we've only known each other for only a couple of hours, but I don't believe you're the kind of person who'd let half a city get blown up."

"How can you know that?"

He smiled knowingly again and turned back to the arcade. "Intuition. Remember? I'm pretty good with these things."

She stared after him. "You're weird."

He laughed. "Says the girl from another world." He paused halfway through the door, then threw her a set of keys. "It's a long way. You can take the blue car parked out back."

She fumbled to catch the keys, eventually letting them slip through her fingers and clatter to the ground. "Are you sure?"

"Location is programmed into the GPS." His back was to her, but she could hear the smile in his voice. "Just tell it where you want to go, and it'll guide you there. Oh, and check the trunk. There might be something useful in there."

Margaret stared at the keys in her hands before looking to Ray. The door had nearly closed behind him when Margaret called out, "Wait!"

He turned back to her. She pulled out the small paper bag of arcade tokens and tossed it to him. "Guess we never did end up playing."

He caught the bag with ease and looked at it for second. "Doesn't mean we still can't." He tossed it back. "You'll just have to come back."

"Even if I don't belong here?"

"Meh," he shrugged. "No one ever really belongs anywhere."

Paper crinkled and coins jingled. She liked the sound of that. "Thank you."

"Good luck, Margaret."

The arcade doors closed with a sense of finality. Her eyes drifted up to the bright sign that faded between colours. ARCADE. It looked lonely in the quiet streets, but she knew that people were inside, getting ready to defend their city once again.

She didn't linger.

■—■—■—■□■—■—■—■

A few more tweaks and the little contraption sprang up. Eight spindly legs twitched, connected to a thin body with an orb that resembled a light bulb. Slowly, the orb started to glow with an ethereal green light not unlike the aura of an open portal.

The man in the white coat nodded to himself as the glowing mechanical spider crawled over the workbench and explored. He adjusted a knob on a control box, and the spider responded. It started spinning a glowing green web, and reality warped around the silk, ripples arching out as the fictional world was altered.

Satisfied with the result, he deactivated it. The spider curled its legs around the orb and the glow faded. The man dropped the little spider into a jar with a dozen other mechanical spiders.

"The preparations are complete," he whispered to himself as he screwed the lid on. "It took longer than expected, but I suppose one gets rusty when out of the game for so long."

He pulled out a case from under the workbench and flicked it open. He tucked the jar away with all its little creatures, then turned to the reason he had to put up with a plasma-obsessed brat for an entire week.

His greatest achievement. Smaller than he had originally planned, but so much more complex than anything he'd ever created. It had been hard to find a fictional world that would support this kind of technology, and he'd had to put up with enough annoyances to complete it, but he'd finally done it!

He let his fingers trace over the spirals and gears as the excitement flooded him. If there was any good that had come from his imprisonment, it was that it had given him lots and *lots* of time to think, re-think, and perfect his design. His theory was sound, and all that was left to do was execute the final test. This time it would work, and it would bring him one step closer to restoring what was lost.

His thoughts drifted to the woman; she was little more than a girl. He'd left her, no doubt confused, back in reality. A rash thing to do, bad mannered even, but how could anyone refute the results?

His seeds had managed to find the Print while he'd been trapped, and he'd been so elated when the transmission had come through that he couldn't help but rush to test his theory.

He wondered what she would think of it—of his ambition.

He placed his grand achievement in the case alongside the jar and his other gadgets. As he was about to close it, another mechanical creature caught his eye. He had made many during his time in this world—most to placate the child villain—but he'd forgotten that he'd thrown this one together.

It was a little sparrow, soldered together from scraps of chaos. He blew off bits of dust and metal flakes from the interlocking plates and exposed cogs. He smiled at it, and with the flick of a finger, he activated the switch on its underbelly. The gears started to turn, and the motor whirred to life. The wings twitched for a moment, and the eyes lit up with a soft yellow light. The small bird jumped to its feet and chirped a sweet tune. The wings started to flap, and it lifted off his hand and flew around his head before landing gently on his shoulder.

He watched the artificial creature as it bounced and chirped, and he smiled wistfully. "Yes, suits her quite well," he concluded. The bird hopped in agreement, and he flicked the case closed.

The tails of his white coat danced in the currents of the automatic doors as he left Heinsrick's base.

CHAPTER 9

BAD GUYS ENJOY COOKIES AT THEIR TEAM MEETINGS

She was overthinking. How exactly did she manage to get herself into this situation? What brought her to this moment? Was it deciding to go find Maître herself after seeing him on TV with Heinsrick? Was it following the villain back into the book after finding the spare Portal Generator? Or was it back when she agreed to accompany the man in the white coat on fantastical adventures?

Really, what had she been thinking?

What did she know about this man? He used to be partners with Uncle Ken (who may or may not have been crazy) but was betrayed and locked into an old book. In hindsight, she should have asked more questions about that.

As soon as she had the chance, she'd ask what really happened between Maître and Ken.

Her white-knuckled grip on the flying car's steering wheel led her to where she could find the man in the white coat. Driving wasn't much different from a regular car... at least while going horizontally. Once the navigation system started telling her to 'Ascend 100 meters, then continue EAST,' her anxiety may have spiked.

Though, amazingly, the car's computer had given her a tutorial. It was some mandatory thing that had to be presented to all newly registered drivers, because apparently, she was a registered driver!

She'd been in a hurry and skipped through most of the video, and she was regretting it. At least the city was on lockdown and there wasn't anyone else out for her to crash into. All she had to worry about was not driving right into the buildings and keeping the stupid machine in the air.

Her shoulders started relaxing as she got the hang of it, but she couldn't quite look down. After the whole getting pushed off a building thing, she found her heart pounding at the thought of being so far off the ground, and it became hard to breathe.

"Continue to your destination on your RIGHT in 200 meters," the GPS informed her.

The outskirts of the city were decrepit. The buildings weren't as tall, and they weren't made of the same pristine glass that the rest of the city had. Instead, they were a mix of dark coloured materials, reinforced concrete, and hard plastics. The ground level looked even worse. The streets were deserted, trash littered the pavement, and the street-side shops were all boarded up. A streetlamp flickered and she shivered when it burnt out. She hoped the sun would hurry up and rise.

The GPS guided her to a small landing that stuck out from a dark grey building that was sandwiched between other buildings. In the darkness, she'd nearly missed it.

Her landing was… not so graceful. The car slammed down loudly on the platform when she flicked off the engine too soon. She groaned as she stumbled out and winced at the cracks in the plastic lining.

Hopefully Ray wouldn't mind…

She shook the thought from her head.

Focus.

The entrance to Heinsrick's lair was before her. It wasn't what she had expected. She'd expected something big and towering—intimidating. In reality, it looked like the entrance to an old hotel with rotating glass doors.

It was framed by an overhang that cast it into darkness, and even though it didn't look like much, it felt like an ominous aura was oozing from it.

Margaret took a deep breath and stepped forward. Even though it was old, the glass doors spun soundlessly and spat her out into a long, dimly lit hallway.

"Please be here."

■—■—■—■ ■ ⬜ ■—■—■—■

In the depths of Heinsrick's lair, four individuals sat around a table in a room dimly lit by a single fluorescent orb that hung suspended in the air and cast deep shadows in every corner.

"This month's meeting of Heinsrick's Henchman, further known as H^2, is now in session," a man said as he laid his robotic hand on the table. The light gleamed off his metallic parts, emphasizing where machine met the cyborg's flesh half. His face was serious as he overlooked the other members. He was not their leader, but it was he who had taken charge since he doubted any of the others would be capable.

"Can we, like, just get this over with," a teenaged girl with long black hair sighed irritably. Her feet were propped up on the table and she flicked the page of her magazine. She wished it was brighter. "I've got somewhere to be and it's way too early for this anyway."

"Master Heinsrick is closer than ever to achieving his goal. As members of H^2, we must be ready to support him," the cyborg enforced sternly.

"I don't even have a shift here today," the girl muttered and slouched further into her chair. She grabbed the floating orb and brought it closer so she could see the pages better.

"You know, I honestly don't know why you even bother to show up," the third member barked. He was no more than a boy, and his voice squeaked with the beginnings of puberty. "It's not like you even do anything."

"Can it, squirt," the teenager shot back.

"What was that?" The boy jumped up onto the table, pulling out a knife. The girl threw the light orb at him in retaliation, and he shrieked as the surprise attack knocked his blade away, and he fell back off the table into his seat.

"Enough! Both of you!" The cyborg tried to restore order and pried the knife from where it had stabbed the table. This was why he had to take charge, because the other members were too immature to do anything on their own. He was met with mumbles and glares as the two children quieted down.

"My, my," the final member of H² laughed and placed a feeble hand to her wrinkled cheek. "You youngsters are always so full of energy. Here, have a cookie." The elderly lady pulled a plate of cookies from out of nowhere and set them on the table.

"Aw, yeah!" The boy sprung forward and nabbed one, shoving half of it in his mouth and reaching for a second. "I don't know how you do it, Granny Tammy, but you always got the goods," he spewed crumbs everywhere.

The teenager picked out a cookie without looking up from her magazine.

The old lady smiled warmly. To the cyborg, she was the biggest mystery of H². Maybe it was the way she could make anyone lower their guard that set off alarms in the cyborg's head, but while he felt like he shouldn't trust her, she hadn't actually done anything other than supply baked goods and mishear what people were saying. He often wondered how she came to be employed under Master Heinsrick, but no one seemed to be able to tell him. Honestly, he was half convinced that she had just wandered in one day, gotten lost, and had no idea what was actually going on. He didn't understand why Master Heinsrick kept her around. They weren't related... at least, he didn't think they were.

"As I was saying..." The cyborg shook himself from his own thoughts and tried to bring the meeting to order again. "It's a critical time, and we have to be on top of our game. Now, has everyone finished their latest traps?" He looked around the room. The boy nodded vigorously, the girl rolled her eyes but nodded, and Granny Tammy continued to knit a pair of socks.

"Good," the cyborg nodded. "Be sure they're fully operational by sunrise. With all that's going on, I have a feeling we'll be dealing with Mecha Arms before long."

"I'd like to see him *try* to get through my room. He'll end up stabbed so many times, you won't even be able to count the number of holes." The boy bounced in his chair manically. He liked stabbing things.

"Very good," the cyborg praised and turned to the teenager. "How're the water tanks holding up?"

"Just fine," she responded without looking up. "I've worked out all the bugs from the moving platforms, and those things that White Coat built are half decent, all things considered."

"He's a weirdo," the boy agreed. "He doesn't come to our meetings, but he sure knows how to make stuff work."

"Speaking of White Coat," the cyborg said. "It seems he's taken his leave."

"You mean he's not even sticking around for the final showdown?" The boy jumped up again.

"Aw, I kind of liked him," the teenager sighed. "He was funny."

"Only because he's a wuss who's all polite to girls." The boy rolled his eyes. "A real man takes control and stabs it 'til it bleeds!"

"Kay, ew."

"Whatever happens to him from now on is no longer our concern," the cyborg said. "Our arrangement has come to an end, and we can go our separate ways and concentrate on the future."

"Yeah, whatever." The teenager flicked the page.

"Well, I think a nice roasted ham would go splendidly with that," Granny Tammy spoke up. "Perhaps some cherry cobbler for dessert? Oh, but where can we find cherries this time of year?"

There was a beat of silence, broken only by the clacking of knitting needles.

"Do her hearing aids need new batteries again?" the boy asked.

"My sensors indicate they do," the cyborg confirmed. He sighed and wiped his hand over his face. "Moving on," he tried again.

Blaring alarms and bright red lights interrupted him. The cyborg let his head fall in defeat.

"Ugh, really?" The teenager covered her ears.

"Kara, what's wrong?" the cyborg asked.

"Intruder alert," the building's AI answered simply.

"Turn off the stupid alarms!" the boy yelled as his voice cracked.

"Where?" The cyborg hadn't expected the heroes to retaliate so soon. They should be scouring the city for the bomb, not attacking their lair.

"The intruder has reached the inner chambers."

"And you're only telling us now!"

"If I recall, the last time I triggered the alarms, I was told not to because the noise was 'TOTALLY OFFSETTING MY VIBES.' So, I let the intruder set off their own alarms."

"Useless computer!" the boy raged.

"Well," the cyborg calmly folded his hands together on the table to try to appear in control. He was very used to complications and annoyances such as these, and over the years, he'd learned to work with them. "It looks like we'll be using our trap rooms sooner than we'd thought."

■—■—■—■◻■—■—■—■

Margaret couldn't help but marvel at the sheer size of the place. She craned her head up to look at the sloping ceiling that was so far away, which seemed completely unnecessary in her opinion, but was nonetheless impressive.

The hallway had opened into a large room that was once a hotel reception area. There was a large unoccupied desk, a set of coat hangers, hallways leading off in all directions, and an elevator behind the desk. All that was missing was a rack of pamphlets and brochures and—no, there it was. Right beside the coat rack.

She smiled dryly.

There was no one around. She wasn't sure how she'd feel if there *was* someone, seeing as she was sneaking into a villain's lair. Although was sneaking really the right word to use? It wasn't like she was trying to hide, and the front door wasn't locked. But… since Heinsrick was out trying to blow up the city, was there even anyone else around to catch her?

Hm. But hadn't Maître been *with* Heinsrick on the building with the bomb? Would he come back here? Oh man, had he already left? Why hadn't she thought of that sooner?

She turned to look back the way she'd come and debated leaving then and there. But… Ray had told her to come here.

Might as well check the place out.

She rummaged around the reception desk because she could. It was mostly papers with doodles and some sticky notes with reminders and… threats?

- FIX VENDING MACHINE
- 2nd FLOOR SINK BACKED UP AGAIN
- WHOEVER KEEPS USING MY KNIFE TO CLEAN OUT THE
  SINK THAT'S BACKED UP, IF I FIND YOU, YOU'LL SPEND THE
  REST OF YOUR LIFE WITH AN EYE PATCH!!!!
- TRY NEW BROWNIE RECIPE

The notes were all written in different handwriting. So, there *were* other people here. She racked her brain for the limited knowledge she had of the world of Mecha Arms but…

Nothing. Not a fandom she was a part of.

That aside, where were these other people? Maybe they could tell her which of the six hallways would lead her to her companion. This was going to be harder than she thought.

She shuffled around the clutter and found a screen built into the surface of the desk.

"Nice."

There was no mouse or keyboard, so she tapped the screen. It lit up with a black and grey design with a big 'H' in the middle. Heinsrick's logo? Do villains get logos?

It prompted her to enter a password.

"Or not."

She let the screen go dark. She didn't want to trigger any alarms. She'd seen, or *read*, too many times about what happens after too many failed attempts. With her luck, it would be lasers or robots that'd try to kill her… or push her off the building. She suddenly remembered that this 'hotel' wasn't on ground level. She imagined a trap door opening beneath her feet and sending her shooting down a slide that would pitch her outside to fall to her death.

"Okay, stop it brain." She leaned against the desk and acknowledged the fact that getting pushed off a building may have permanently trauma-tized her.

She dug a metal bead out of her utility belt and rolled it between her fingers in an attempt to calm her mind. Fidgeting had always helped. She'd found the little beads in the trunk of the blue car. Ray had told her that there may be some useful stuff in there. She'd been quite surprised to find a small stash of gadgets and a belt to carry them. She didn't take all of it, but these little EMP beads seemed small and light enough.

The car's computer system had explained how they work when she'd picked them up: throw them, and they would send out an electromagnetic pulse that would disable anything mechanical within a certain radius. She could kind of understand what it was talking about, but she skipped over the science and focused on the part that said they would be able to stop robots from killing her.

Some other gadgets she grabbed included a ray gun, a grappling hook, and X-ray glasses. They were the easiest and least complicated things to understand. The computer started explaining the other more complicated things, but it was beyond her. Instead of accidentally lighting herself on fire, she'd stick with the basics.

The problem now was that she still didn't know where to go. Leaning against the reception desk, she considered the X-ray glasses. Maybe she could see where Maître was by looking through the walls. Wouldn't hurt to try.

She put them on. A small button on the rim activated them, and a schematic of the building appeared, outlining all the rooms and floors around, above, and below her.

All the lines and shades of colours mixed together, overlaying all the rooms on top of each other. Her eyes lost focus, and all sense of perception vanished. She stumbled, losing her balance even though she was standing still.

She ripped the glasses off.

"Nope," she muttered, bracing herself on the desk and riding out the dizzy spell. She had been able to look through the walls, and the walls beyond that, and the next ones, until there was just too much information to take in. She'd lost all sense of where she was, what was actually in front of her, and what was further away.

Would it be better to wait for someone to notice her? Was there anyone there to notice her? Heinsrick *was* out trying to blow up the city in… How long had it been?

She glanced at her watch. Two hours. It'd already been that long? She thought about how time passed here. Was it the same as the real world? What if there was some sort of time dilation and she ended up missing opening day? Wait—did she leave the front door open? Was she going to get robbed?

Stop! Focus! She slapped her cheeks. *I'm here to find Maître and get some answers.*

Deep breath in… and out…

Gotta solve my problems myself. Can't keep waiting for someone to show up and do it for me. Wait, there!

She scurried over to the elevator behind the desk where, plastered on the wall, there was a conveniently located map of the facility. The name of the hotel had been scratched out and 'Secret Lair' written overtop in magic marker. She resisted the urge to facepalm. It was no wonder Ray knew exactly where to find this place. How did she not see this before?

The building was a maze of hallways and numerous rooms that used to be hotel rooms. Now, they mostly seemed to be abandoned. As she ascended to each subsequent floor, she saw that the original plans had been corrected with more marker as renovations, she guessed, had taken place.

Her eyes skimmed past rooms labelled Shark Room, Plasma Chamber, and The Room That Shall Not Be Named! It was as ridiculous as the rest of this place. She eventually found something worth checking out.

Security was on the fourth floor. Hopefully, there were cameras she could use to find him.

She called the elevator and it opened with a pleasant '*ding.*'

"You have selected FOURTH FLOOR," a woman's automated voice announced.

The door closed silently, and she felt the floor move beneath her as the elevator began its ascension. A soft, enjoyable tune played over the speaker, and she tapped her foot unconsciously to the beat. Had she ever been in an elevator that actually played music before?

The thought had barely passed through her head when the elevator ground to a halt so fast that her feet left the floor. She crashed to the floor as metal shrieked and groaned at the sudden stop.

"Oh great, what now?" She gripped the handrail and hauled herself back up to her feet.

Pressing the 'open door' button didn't do anything. Neither did smashing any of the other buttons. All it did was raise her anxiety for the hundredth time since coming to this world.

"Come on, come on."

Everything had shut down, but at least the lights hadn't gone out.

As a last-ditch effort, she tried jamming her fingers in between the doors and prying them open. She struggled for half a minute before deciding that either the elevators were stronger than the ones in reality, or TV has been lying about them all along.

She didn't have to stew in her own mind for long, though.

"Welcome to Heinsrick HQ," the lady's voice sounded again.

She felt some of the tension bleed away at the announcement. That meant there were people here. They'd be able to help her.

"We apologize for the delay, but as a security breach, you are not authorized to go any further."

"Wai—what?"

"Please be patient while our security team prepares their countermeasures."

"Countermeasures!" she squeaked. "No, no, no, no, no, no, you don't understand. I'm just looking for—"

"Please refrain from back talking and remain patient while our security team prepares countermeasures."

It answered her. Was she talking to a person? Or an AI?

"Wh-what kind of countermeasures?" she asked.

"The members of H² have prepared various rooms containing different trials. Your task, should you wish to continue, is to clear each room and continue deeper into the facility."

"Really?" she asked, dumbfounded. "You're not gonna just, like, send some guards with guns to escort me out?"

"Guards have proven to be ineffective against past intruders."

"Right, 'cause the only people breaking in here are overpowered preteens with mechanical arms," she muttered. "Um, I'm really not a threat though. I'm just looking for my friend? Uh… guy in a white coat?"

"Please refrain from asking useless questions and wait patiently while our security team prepares countermeasures."

She sighed. "Great."

CHAPTER 10

IT'S BETTER FOR EVERYONE IF YOU DON'T MAKE ME MAD

Margaret stewed in her anxiety. A few minutes into it, she was startled by the AI's voice again.

"Thank you for your continued patience. The counter-measures have been completed, and you may begin your first trial."

The elevator doors dinged open. Margaret stepped out into a dark room and squinted into the gloom. Water was splashing, and the smell of chlorine was thick in the air.

The lights snapped on.

"Allow me to introduce the first trial, created by Synthesizer, the first member of H²."

Her eyes adjusted, and she found herself in a large, open room, complete with a full swimming pool. Splashing around in the water was—

Wait, were those…

The mechanical monsters jumped out of the water, bodies arching perfectly before splashing back into the pool.

"Robot sharks," she swallowed. "Naturally."

She started to tremble because of *course* robots are a thing here too.

A screech pierced the air as a microphone turned on. A bored voice started talking.

"Yeah, so it's pretty simple."

The speaker was set up on the other side of the room where a balcony overlooked the pool. A teenaged girl with long black hair was slumped over the rail with a magazine dangling over the edge. She had a PA microphone propped up on the rail beside her.

"Survive the shark tank and make it to the other side of the room and through the door to win," Synthesizer said in the same bored tone. "The platforms will start to move along set paths. Use those to get across while dodging the sharks or whatever." She brought the magazine up to her face again. "Good luck, or something."

Margaret stood frozen as the buzzer sounded and sharks jumped out of the water again, clearing the four platforms that floated in the water. The platforms then started to move in seemingly random directions.

"Initiating trial."

She looked around desperately. They couldn't be serious. Someone was going to pop out and tell her this was all just a big joke! How was she supposed to—

"Agh!" She fell back as a shark rammed itself into the side of the pool where she was standing. Her legs gave out, and she scrambled back along the floor. "Are you serious?"

Was she *really* supposed to jump onto moving platforms in a shark-infested swimming pool? There had to be another way. Just think. Think—

Wait.

"Um…" Her voice cracked and she cleared her throat. "Uh, hey!"

"What?" Synthesizer asked, annoyed. The microphone crackled.

"I can, uh, do whatever I want as long as I get to the other side, right?"

"'S'what I said."

"Okay." Margaret nodded to herself. She eyed the shark tank and picked herself up off the floor. Then, carefully, she inched toward the side of the room where there was a clear ledge, completely traversable, around the entire outside of the pool. The pool itself was more rounded than square; it was probably the hotel's pool before it was rebuilt into this death trap. But there was clearly room to walk around it.

"I'll just…" she said loud enough for the teenager to hear, "go this way."

She started to inch around the tank, keeping a shoulder against the wall to stay as far away from the water as possible. The platforms kept moving steadily across the rippling water as the sharks swam beneath the surface. They were mean looking, with layer after layer of metal sheets overlapping in a way that let the monsters bend and move their fins. Their beady red eyes pierced through the water like lasers, and their teeth were sharp enough to bite through steel… or so she imagined. It was something she'd rather not test.

They jumped again. Too close to where she was. Margaret's eyes widened, and she screamed as the hulking beasts loomed over her. They splashed harmlessly back into the water. For good measure, one of the sharks rammed its head into the side of the pool as if it were angry that it hadn't gotten a good shot at eating her.

Her legs gave out and she slid down the wall. Sweet son of a banshee, that was too close. But she couldn't stop, so she started to crawl. She splashed in the little puddles at the pool's edge and tried her hardest not to slip, but she made it to the other side without further incident.

Minor heart attack and possible new phobia aside, she braced herself against the far wall and somehow climbed back to her feet.

"Huh," Synthesizer said from above her. "Never thought of that. Whatever. You pass."

Wait, seriously?

The elevator she was propped up against slid open and she fell back through it. She laid there for a moment, just staring at the ceiling.

At least that Synthesizer girl didn't seem to care that she'd used a loophole. She hoped the rest of the 'trials' would be along the same lines.

"Hah, yeah right." She tried not to get her hopes up.

"You have completed the first trial. Please continue to the next room."

"How many of these trials did you say there were?" she asked, sitting up and scootching back to lean against the wall as the elevator doors closed. She needed a moment to calm her heartrate and even out her breathing.

"There are a total of four members of H². You have completed one trial. Three remain."

"Great," Margaret sighed as the elevator dinged and the door opened to the next floor. She stood up and shook off the lingering jitters from the last trial. A long hallway stretched out before her and ended with a door. There was no doorknob, and for a second, she wasn't sure if she was supposed to do something. Then the door swooshed open on its own.

The room beyond was pitch black, but this time she was ready when the blinding lights snapped on.

A cackling laughter echoed around the large, mostly empty metallic room. She couldn't tell where it was coming from.

She looked around the room, wary of what deadly tricks might pop out this time. The whole room, from one end to the other, was empty. It looked safe to walk across to the next door except for the little holes. They started a few feet into the room and covered every inch of the floors and walls. The only question was what would come flying out to impale her.

She took a cautious step into the room and the elevator closed.

Like the previous room, a balcony was set above the next door, and standing on the ledge of the balcony with a PA microphone in his hand was a kid even younger than Heinsrick who was laughing like a maniac.

"I introduce the second trial, created by Zap, the second member of H²."

"I get it, they go in order," Margaret muttered. "What even *is* H²? A group of kids following around an evil genius brat bent on destroying the world? Honestly, are there *no* adults in this world?"

"All the grownups are too busy working and doing *taxes*," Zap mocked. "They don't care what we do, as long as we don't track mud into the house on the way home for dinner."

"Someone definitely doesn't hug you enough," she deadpanned.

Zap grinned. "BEHOLD!" He spread his arms out wide, and his voice echoed despite the microphone being nowhere near his mouth. "The Trial of Impaling!"

"Oh, you named it. How nice," she cringed and eyed the neat rows of little holes again.

The kid activated an unseen mechanism, and from every little hole, a long, sharp, and deadly seven-foot spear with a tip so sharp it hurt just to look at shot out.

Margaret flinched at their sudden appearance. They retracted slowly, metal grinding on metal, and she wondered if this would count as another new phobia or if fear of spontaneous stabbing was just common sense.

Zap twirled the microphone's cord around his finger, still not talking into it. "The spears are controlled by motion sensors so sensitive that even a fly could set it off! NYA HA HA HA HA! All you gotta do is make your way across, but there aren't any obvious loopholes like the last trial. Honestly, Synth is so lazy leaving such an obvious opening like that. I'm so much more reliable; Master Heinsrick should just hurry and make *me* his first!"

A loud buzzer sounded.

"Initiating trial."

The room went silent. She didn't want to step forward. Walking meant death spikes. Death spikes are bad, so moving is bad. In fact, she was quite content to simply not move for as long as it took.

The kid was right. There was no easy path through the spike field. There were even spikes in the *walls*. She'd either have to run very, very fast or just. . . not move at all.

Not moving sounded better.

"You gonna do something?" Apparently, Zap didn't share her opinion. "Move! Do something!" He swung his arms around and the microphone swung with them. Why did he even bother with it? He wasn't actually *using* it. "If you don't start doing something—oops."

And there it went. The microphone flew from his hand, out over the floor, and before it could even hit the ground, multiple spikes of death shot up and stabbed it into a million pieces. More spikes shot up as the pieces scattered before finally stuttering to a stop.

"Whoops."

"Please refrain from damaging company property. The cost has been deducted from your salary."

"Yeah, yeah, I get it. Shut up."

"Please refrain from harassing co-workers. The cost of the lawsuit has been deducted from your salary."

"You're an artificial intelligence! You can't file a lawsuit! And I'd hardly call you a co-worker!"

Margaret only half listened to the kid arguing with the computer. Pieces of the microphone were scattered all over the floor. It got her thinking. She'd never been all that good at science or technology, but she was decent at recognizing patterns and solving puzzles. The microphone had just showed her that this whole room was one big puzzle.

It had broken into multiple pieces, but only one section of spikes had activated at a time. It was only programmed to follow one target at a time. Seemed like a pretty big flaw to overlook. If there was more than one person, then someone's guaranteed to get across.

"Hm…" She patted her pockets before remembering that this jumpsuit didn't have any. She needed something to test her theory. She could try the dumb X-ray glasses, but she'd need more than one thing.

What about…

"What are these?"

"Tokens. Figured you might get bored of just talking to this goof. And if you're looking for a challenge, you know, not to brag or anything, but I'm a god when it comes to Robo-Slayer: Redemption."

…*"Guess we never did end up playing."*

"Doesn't mean we still can't. Just means you'll have to come back."

She pulled the little paper bag from her utility belt. The tokens jangled inside. He'd said that she'd just have to just come back, but she'd probably return to her reality once she met up with Maître… if she survived until then.

With that thought, she flicked a single golden coin out over the playing field. Spears instantly shot up, following the path of the coin as it rolled to the middle of the room. It took about five seconds after they shot up for the spikes to retract. A lot quicker than when the microphone shattered. Interesting.

"What are you doing?" Zap demanded from his perch. Apparently, he was done fighting with the AI. "You're not gonna get across by throwing stuff."

"I'm experimenting!" She snapped. "I'm not superhuman and I'm not suicidal; cut me a break."

"Boo! This is boring! Hurry and get stabbed already!"

"How about no!"

This is impossible. I can't concentrate with him yelling every thirty seconds... Let's try a different approach.

"So, you're like a villain, right?" she asked, hoping that since this was a kids' book, this train of thought might work.

"You have to ask?" Zap flicked his hand. "I'm one of the best villains of our times! Or I will be one day. Second only to Master Heinsrick!"

"Uh, right." She took a breath. "So, if I'm not mistaken, after the villain traps the hero, aren't they supposed to leave them to their fate while going off to enact their final plan?"

"Carl says I'm not supposed to do that anymore," Zap pouted.

"Carl?"

"Stupid cyborg doesn't even know what it means to be a proper villain."

"Carl the cyborg. Right. So, this Carl's like your boss, then?"

"I only follow Master Heinsrick!"

"But you listen to Carl?"

". . . I don't have to listen to him! You're right!"

Got him, she smiled. "Yeah, Heinsrick is out there all by himself with the bomb, right?" she encouraged him. "He'll need the help of someone as capable as his number two."

"Well, then." He still looked reluctant to leave. "As much as I'd love to see you get impaled, I have better things to do." He turned his back to her and flourished a cape she only just noticed he was wearing. "Besides, I can always watch the replay footage later. Smile for the cameras!"

A door whooshed behind him, and she let out a breath of relief. "That's one problem out of the way. Now, how do I get out of this one?" she muttered to herself and looked around the room again.

I wonder if I can just... She glanced at the door she had come through. Could she go back?

"Please note that you must complete the trial to pass to the next stage. Do not get any ideas because you managed to deceive H² member Zap into abandoning his post. And do

not think of running away, as there is no place in this
building where I cannot find you."

She flinched at the monotone robotic voice. *Forgot about the computer.*
"Don't suppose you can turn off the death trap and just let me pass?"

"Negative."

"Didn't think so," she sighed and jangled the bag of tokens. "Got a
bunch of high-tech gadgets but my life is relying on a bag of cheap arcade
tokens. Makes perfect sense."

She flicked another token and flinched at how suddenly the spikes shot
up. It seemed more real now that she didn't have the comedic relief. Could
she really do this? Get across a minefield of death spikes with only a bag of
little gold coins? There had to be a better way.

She liked the 'not moving' strategy but she also didn't like the idea of
staying here any longer than necessary.

The spikes retracted. She took a deep breath. Time to experiment.

Two tokens. She held one in each hand and threw them in opposite
directions. The spikes shot up instantly, but like she thought, they only followed one of the tokens, and it seemed to take a split second longer for
them to react.

Again. Three tokens. The effect was much more pronounced. The
system couldn't figure out what to track. Spikes started triggering at
random, lagging and glitching.

Again and again, she threw more tokens, and little by little, the whole
system started breaking down. At five tokens, one section of spikes failed
to retract. At six, something started sparking and smoking. At seven, she
took a deep breath and sprinted.

She hadn't intended to go at that moment. She didn't think, she may
have screamed— *probably* screamed—but her body moved before her
brain could tell her otherwise.

Metal screeched on metal, sparks flew, and something exploded, but
she crashed face first into the wall on the other side of the room without
daring to slow down or look back. Her face, chest, arms, and pretty much
everything else stung from the sudden impact, but at least she wasn't
riddled with holes.

She braced herself against the wall and turned to look back at the mine-field she had miraculously managed to cross.

Metal had ground on metal, something was still sparking, and about half the floor had actually exploded. Spears stuck out at every angle in a mix of melted plastic and singed metal, and the complex inner workings of the trap were laid bare and destroyed.

Guess arcade tokens trump death spikes, she thought meekly.

"Trial cleared. Please continue to the next room." The AI's voice seemed to ring and echo in her head… or maybe that was the adrenaline.

"Give me a second!" she snapped. She slid down the wall and splayed her legs out in front of her. She needed a moment to process.

Her heart pounded with the absurdity of it all. Honestly, what was she doing? Her chest heaved and shoulders shook from the strain of trying to hold it all in. Wait, why was she holding it in. She let it all out.

"AH HA HA HA!"

Her lungs heaved with laughter and her body jittered with mirth as she let the liquid joy rush through her veins.

I'm losing my mind!

She couldn't find it in herself to care. The adrenaline was melting away and the aches started to settle in. The laughter morphed into a groan, and she slid farther down the wall that she had run right into. She gingerly touched her nose.

"Alright, come on," she told herself and pushed off the wall. The giggles were still bouncing around in her chest, but she got her feet underneath her and straightened up with a mixture of groans and giggles. "Oh, stop being so dramatic," she scolded herself with a grin. "You're not hurt that badly."

"Are you prepared to proceed?"

"Bring it on, robo-wench!"

The door slid open, and she walked down the next hallway without hesitation. She was just about done with all of this.

"Two more to go." She wondered what would be thrown at her next. Giant rolling boulders? A labyrinth with a monster? Hell, a high stakes game of chess to the death?

Her body buzzed with tremors from the adrenaline, and she could feel her hands starting to tremble, but she'd made it this far. No point in turning back now.

She jumped into a jog, and all too soon, the next door slid open. A new wave of anxiety passed through her, and her gut said that this one wasn't going to be like the others.

The lights snapped on. This room was round and full of pillars and blocks arranged randomly around an open space in the middle.

This is a battle arena, her mind supplied. Her gut dropped.

"Introducing the third trial, created by Carl, the third member of H²."

Instead of a balcony, the creator of the trial appeared from the floor. A hole opened in the middle of the room, smoke billowed out, and a figure rose. The light glinted off metal prosthetics and his deep brown skin as the cyborg grinned at her.

"The time for childish games is over," Carl the cyborg announced.

"Hey look, an adult!" Her eyebrows rose in surprise. "Must be hard dealing with crazed children all day long."

The cyborg tilted his head and considered her. "It is."

"But you'd think that you'd at least *try* to come up with a villain name. I mean, Carl? Why use your real name? It's not scary!" Yeah, she left her filter back at the spike room.

"'Carl *is* my villain name." The cyborg's eye twitched.

"Wai—wait, hold up." She held up her hands. "You *chose* the name 'Carl?'"

Carl the scary cyborg took a deep, calming breath. "You managed to outsmart the system so far, but this time there *is* no system. There's nothing you can exploit. No shortcuts, no glitches. The only way you're making it past this trial is by proving yourself in battle."

Her throat went dry as he confirmed her suspicion. "Uh…"

"You may use whatever weapon and fighting style you wish," he continued, ignoring her. "Since you seem to have a way of flirting around the rules, the only one is to win. Anything goes."

"I don't—I mean, but—" she stuttered as her earlier stupor evaporated. "Dah, I'm not—I don't fight!"

"Then why are you carrying a weapon?" Carl scolded. Her hand went to the ray gun at her hip. "Weapons are meant for fighting. They're not there to look pretty; they're for action! *So, let's see you use them.*"

"Initiating trial."

All too quickly, the cyborg disappeared back into the ground, and panels started opening up along the walls. Suddenly, there were drones circling around the pillars with deadly propellers spinning loudly and gun turrets rotating into position underneath.

From hidden speakers, Carl's voice echoed, "Prove yourself."

"Round one: Start."

I'd really rather not! She barely had the chance to think before the chaos started.

Beams of what she could only imagine were plasma shot from the drone fighters' turrets and blasted the wall directly behind her. The shock wave pitched her forward, and she screamed because *apparently*, they were starting!

"Frak!" She yelled and scurried with her hands and feet to the cover of the closest pillar where she cowered in a tight ball with her arms covering her head. "Okay, okay, okay." She uncurled a little. The buzzing of the drone fighters didn't follow her, so she peeked out from behind the pillar.

She counted ten of them hovering in formation around the trap door that *Carl the freaking cyborg* had appeared and disappeared from. Irritatingly, it was marked with a big, tacky 'H.' The fighters were only circling in the air, as if waiting for her to make the first move.

Or giving me a chance to prepare and gather my thoughts.

The cyborg hadn't seemed overly hostile... well, as hostile as sending plasma robot drones after her. More like encouraging her. Testing her.

Well duh! That's the point of a trial!

Stop it, you're getting sidetracked. First things first. She grabbed the small ray gun and inspected it. It was the only thing she had to fight with. She flicked a button she assumed was the safety and was rewarded when it started glowing as it powered up. She held it to her chest with both hands while she centered herself. "Just point and shoot."

Another second and she leapt from her cover and took aim.

Unfortunately, but somehow not surprisingly, the drones were faster. The closest drone fired first and hit the ground at her feet. She stumbled back, cursing, and her shot went wide and blasted a section of one of the pillars to rubble.

She sprinted to the next obstacle while shooting in the general direction of the drones. She didn't hit anything.

Okay, okay, she puffed from the mild exertion. *Aiming is important. But at least this thing can do some damage.*

She let her guard down and a drone buzzed into view. It had followed her! The turret rotated into position and charged up.

"Mother of—" She fell onto her face, and the shot went over her head. Another drone came from behind, and she rolled as she fumbled with the ray gun. She managed to get off a shot that glanced off the second drone's propellers. It careened into a wall and clattered to the ground.

Guess they're not *just gonna wait for me*, she thought bitterly and ran for another pillar. She shot while she ran and tried that aiming thing. The other drones swerved out of the way and scattered around the room.

All bets were off. The fight had begun, and she was out of her depth. She'd never been a fighter—even in the few RPGs she'd played, she'd always preferred range over melee, staying away from the thick of things.

Was there a way for her to get away? No, they'd all scatter. There was no 'safe' space where she could pick off the enemies.

"Come on." She ground her teeth together and crouched behind a waist-high barrier as a shot of plasma crashed into it. She popped up again, braced her arms against the barrier, and shot three times in succession before the drone could charge up its next shot. She missed all three.

"Come on!" she shouted in frustration and took cover again. Another drone circled around behind her, and she fired blindly, again missing her intended target but miraculously hitting one on the other side of the room. The unsuspecting drone was blasted to pieces.

She was running again. *This isn't working. I'm a terrible, horrible shot! I can take them out in one shot, but that doesn't matter if I can't hit them!*

She dove behind a taller wall and tried to catch her breath as she listened to the movements of the drone fighters retreating and starting to patrol around the room again.

Her breath shook. She leaned heavily against the wall.

What do I do? Her brain looped and her heart hammered. *Think, think, think! What do I know about battling in books?... Each book is different! If I knew more about Mecha Arms—but I don't! Don't dwell on 'what ifs.' What can I do as I am now?*

She fumbled with her belt, trying to remember what she had. She pulled out one of the small metallic beads.

"Oh yeah." She smiled, getting giddy and feeling the hysteria sinking in.

A drone buzzed directly overhead and startled her. She fell back on her butt before composing herself and throwing the EMP bead at it. Like her shooting, her throwing wasn't any better. The bead didn't hit the drone, but it didn't need to. The bead activated, and a sphere of electricity arched through the air. The drone fighters within range shut down and fell to the ground.

The closest one fell right beside her, and she wasted no time blasting it in its stupid face. The ray pierced through the metal, and at such a close range, it left a perfectly round hole straight through.

"Alright." She smiled, pulling out another EMP bead with a shaking hand. "Maybe I can brain my way out after all."

She came out from her cover and noticed another drone that had been hit by the first bead. She closed the gap and finished that one off too.

Okay, okay, two more down. She nodded to herself. *However freaking many more to go. I can do this. Let's go!*

She followed the sound of the drone propellers and found two. They engaged as she drew close, and their turrets started to charge. She took cover behind a pillar, and they both discharged their plasma. The pillar broke at her back. She didn't have time to move, and the rubble crumbled on top of her.

She struggled to free herself as two more drones joined the others. Together, they all charged their turrets.

She flicked a metal bead towards the group, and the electricity erupted around them. One misfired and took out one of its own before it self-destructed from the strain. The other two fell as their systems tried to reboot.

5TE

Two more down, she counted off and strained to move the rocks pinning her down.

Something shifted, and she was able to wiggle out only to come face to face with a fully charged turret. She ducked down, pressing her face into the dusty ground just as the plasma scorched her back, only narrowly missing the lethal shot.

She slammed another EMP into the ground in front of her and felt her hair prickle from the static as the drone clattered to the ground. She dug the ray gun from the rubble and blasted it in its stupid face. It exploded, and she slumped back to try and catch her breath.

She didn't get long. Propellers started whirring again as two drones finished rebooting, systems fully operational.

"Crap!" She'd noticed too late. Their turrets were charged. She turned to run, but there was no cover.

Which direction? Agh, no time—just go!

She pitched forward, and she felt it hit. The plasma bore into her back, two shots that sent her flying, crashing into the ground, and rolling across the floor until she came to a sudden stop against the wall.

She didn't move. It felt like she was on fire.

What now? What can I do? Is there anything I can do? I got hit. It hurts. Did I lose? Am I going to die? Can I even die in a book? What happens if I do?

Wait—

She furrowed her brow, her tormented inner thoughts interrupted. She shifted and arched her back. It stung, but did the shot really do all that much damage? She rose to her hands and knees and stretched an arm to feel where she'd been hit.

Yes, it hurt, but it hadn't broken the skin. Heck, it didn't even rip her clothes! But how?

Don't tell me, she groaned internally, kind of annoyed, but tried to convince herself not to be too mad. After all, this was the logic, or *rules*, of this fictional world. This was a children's book, and in these types of books, no matter how many times the hero is hit, they always get back up and keep fighting. It was unrealistic and one of her pet peeves.

So, she cautiously stood up, testing how her limbs moved, and found that she could ignore the throbbing without too much trouble.

It irked her.

"Well, what's the point of that!" she yelled at the remaining drones that still flew around. What's the point of struggling if there's no consequences? How's a hero supposed to grow if they never lose because they can always get back up? It's stupid! It's childish! It's unrealistic! It pissed her off!

The two drones that had shot her closed in again for another try.

"No!" she scolded and threw an EMP bead. It soared through the air and smacked one of them square in the face. Electricity arched, and she was running before they even hit the ground. She shot them both point blank. Then, she screamed and kept shooting.

"Stupid books! With their stupid logic!" She kept yelling as she turned the ray gun on the environment and shot every pillar that was left standing. It may not have been the smartest move, but it was cathartic, and she was done hiding. "Where's the next one!" She spun around the ruined room, but there were no more. The last of the drones had been crushed by her onslaught of falling pillars and were buried in the resulting chaos.

The corpses of ten fighter drones sparked lifelessly on the ground, some more intact than others.

"Round one: complete."

"Oh yeah! Who's buzzing now—wait! *Round one?*"

"Round two: start."

A door slid open, and a giant armoured robo-beast that looked like a bear stormed out and roared.

"Seriously!" she screamed back and stamped her foot.

The beast reared on its hind legs and towered over her. Like the sharks, it was made of multiple overlapping panels with exposed gears and beady red eyes. She found it hard to believe that the 'no injury' thing applied to teeth and claws.

The new enemy roared and charged forward. She fired a few shots at it before her instincts took over and her legs started moving. The next thing she knew, she was on the other side of the room, and the robo-bear crashed into the wall. She had a few moments before it started charging at her again. She dug around the pouch, and her chest tightened when she found there was only one EMP bead left. She pulled it out and stared at it with wide eyes.

Only one left.

All or nothing. There better not be any more after this. She swallowed nervously as the robot roared again.

She didn't think. She breathed. The bead soared through the air as she raised her gun at the charging bear. The bead exploded and hit the robot. It shuddered and groaned against the barrage of electricity, but its body was a lot bigger than the drones. The effect wasn't enough to bring it down. But its momentum had stopped.

She let out what she hoped was a battle cry and fired her gun as she ran toward it. It was too late to turn around.

Her shots went wide, hitting only half the time and nothing vital. The bear creaked and groaned as its processors fought the surges of electricity, and it reared up to its hind legs.

She was right in front of it. Too close to miss. She fired into its chest. Again and again and again. Sections of metal plating snapped off and exposed circuits started sparking. She aimed a little higher, up towards the head, and continued shooting.

Something exploded.

She froze with her ray gun still outstretched, heart pounding painfully and breath ravaging her throat. The neck of the robot was smoking in the absence of its head.

For a second, it was quiet.

Then, the monster teetered forward and fell.

Right on top of her.

She tried to get out of the way, but while her brain was screaming, her body refused to move.

The robot bear crashed down, crushing her underneath it.

The weight was too much. She couldn't move, and she must have hit her head because everything started going fuzzy and darkening around the edges.

Her eyes slipped closed as the computer's voice announced her victory.

"Round two: complete."

CHAPTER 11

HOW AM I SUPPOSED TO KNOW WHAT'S RIGHT?

The villain stood on the platform overlooking the city that would soon be reduced to nothing. Something about this scheme felt different from all the others before. It seemed more final, like he might actually succeed.

"Only two hours left," Tidus Heinsrick said to the world as he soaked up the last view of the city that he would ever see.

"Master Heinsrick." The call connected to his modulator and broke him from his thoughts.

"Yes, what is it, Carl?" he answered. He couldn't be annoyed at the distraction. The finality of everything had brought a sense of tranquility to him.

"We've apprehended an intruder."

"They went to our base? Why?"

"Not the heroes, Master. A woman."

"Woman?"

"She claims to be looking for White Coat."

"Oh!" Heinsrick grinned. "So, she went that far, did she?"

"You know her?"

"Yes. She has something I want. Bring her here. I'm sure she'd be interested in witnessing the final confrontation."

"Master Heinsrick, if I may ask, who is she?"

"A book keeper from the world beyond White Coat's portal. If it weren't for that device she has strapped to her arm, I'd still be stuck on the other side."

"A mere book keeper…"

"What is it?"

"It's just… for a simple bookseller to make it through two of our trials…"

"She did what?"

"Exploiting flaws in both Synthesizer's shark room and Zap's spear challenge, then fighting admirably and clearing two rounds of my own trial despite obviously having no prior battle experience."

"She's got more guts than I gave her credit for. I mean, I figured she had a strong will, but she may turn out to be useful even if she can be annoying."

"Yes, Master Heinsrick."

The call ended and Heinsrick grinned. "Seems like I underestimated you, book keeper."

■—■—■—■◘■—■—■—■

The streets were empty. The clock ticked down the final minutes before detonation. The man in the white coat walked along the sidewalk, flanked by his mechanical spiders that cast an eerie green glow down the empty streets. He stopped in front of a building with a colourful sign.

This was it. The Print was right inside. All those years of experimentation and searching, all coming down to one moment. He finally had the means of opening the Print. Throughout all his adventures, he had never made it this far. Another step toward achieving his true desire.

His white coat caught the wind as he approached the door. His scouts clicked along, scuttling ahead and starting to spin glowing green webs over the entrance. The fabric of the fictional world bent around the webbing and rippled outward.

There it is. His smile spread as he spied the Print through the glass. *So, that's where you've been hiding.* He gave the signal and the spiders moved in.

"Breaking news," the TV in the display window crackled to life. "The timer continues to count down, and it looks like our heroes have discovered the secret location of the Shell of Vengeance. Reporting live."

He paused as the video feed cut away to the confrontation taking place. Tidus Heinsrick faced off against Mecha Arms and Ringlet on a floating platform above City Square. But it wasn't the children that had him pulling up short and stopping his spiders. Behind Heinsrick and directly beside the Shell of Vengeance was a cylindrical plasma prison holding the last person he would have expected to see here.

"Oh, my dear, what have you gotten yourself into?" he muttered.

'It literally fell apart,' Heinsrick had said. The Portal Generator would only have done that if the exertion level had been exceeded by an extreme amount. So, he must have opened the portal, and dear Margaret got dragged back through.

"So, Heinsrick did manage to open the portal." He ran a hand down his face. Regardless of how it happened…

He turned away from the building with the colourful sign, turned away from the Print, turned away from everything he'd been striving towards. He turned away and set his sights on City Square. His new assistant was in trouble.

■—■—■—■□■—■—■—■

Margaret sighed in exasperation as she watched the kids throw childish insults back and forth. They'd been at it for a solid ten minutes, and at this point, there were drones circling around sporting logos from different news stations. She suspected they were purposely stalling, waiting for the rest to get there so their epic battle could be shared with the entire world.

Her mood was further dampened by the fact that the plasma lining her prison muffled all sound so she couldn't hear anything they were saying. So, she decided to come up with her own dialogue.

"Look at me! I'm so great! I crash into people's bookstores and am obsessed with plasma!"

"I'll stop you because I'm the righteous hero, but I'm not gonna do it now 'cause we have to wait until the timer's about to run out before I stop it with only one second left."

"That's not gonna happen because I have *plasma*!"

"Yeah? Well, I have robot arms that can smash your plasma!"

"You fool! Nothing can smash plasma!"

"Watch me!"

"PLASMA!"

"ARMS!"

Suddenly, the two boys jumped towards each other and startled her out of her daydreaming.

"Oh! They're actually starting." She pressed her hands against the plasma shield. The last time these two fought, she'd been too busy cowering behind a car trying not to get caught up in the exchange. But as was demonstrated rather unnecessarily, there wasn't much that could get to her in the plasma prison.

A chunk of stray concrete came flying towards her but crumbled away harmlessly the moment it touched the plasma shield. It was safe to touch from the inside, but instant death from the outside.

She wasn't sure if it was because she had become desensitized over the course of her time here, having to go through those stupid trials, or just the fact that literally nothing could touch her in here, but she didn't feel scared. A little anxious, but not scared.

She watched them fight. It was intense. Heinsrick the madman—the guy who had dragged her on a high-speed car chase and ruthlessly blasted pursuers to nothing. Mecha, the hidden hero, calm and collected—a kid who had decided to trust her despite her apparent affiliation with the enemy. The two couldn't be more different, but they battled in a dance that flowed as naturally as breathing, attacking and countering, gaining the upper-hand and losing it just as quickly.

This was different from picturing a fight scene when reading words on a page or watching it second-hand on a screen. She was so absorbed in it all that she didn't notice the figure sliding up behind her cage until the plasma wall disappeared and she fell back into his arms.

Instantly, the battle was whisked away as the spotless white coat fluttered in the strong winds of the high altitude. The epic fight was background noise to his grin, which sparkled with a bit of madness. Any doubts she'd felt about his motives were whisked away in the heat of the moment.

"You seem to have had quite the adventure, my dear."

"Maître!" She threw her arms around his neck before she could think and snatched them back just as fast. Her face heated up when she realized how close they were to each other, and she scrambled out of his arms.

He quirked an eyebrow, and his lips settled into a small smile as he let it pass. "Come along now, we can't dilly dally."

"Wait, shouldn't we help? What about the bomb that's about to go off?"

"My dear, you forget that we're inside a fictional world. The result of this battle has already been decided. Our meddling won't change that." He held out a hand to her. "Now, shall we get going before this entire platform is destroyed?"

"But didn't you—"

A sudden explosion interrupted her train of thought, and she grabbed his arm to let him whisk her to the edge of the platform where a flying motorcycle was waiting, equipped with a sidecar and everything. She felt her legs start to acquire jelly-like features when she was reminded that they were *very* high up, but she let Maître guide her to the sidecar, holding her hand the whole way. He easily leapt into his own seat and passed her a helmet.

The engine revved, and the tails of his white coat flapped in the wind. They left the noise and battle behind as they descended. Margaret watched the platform shake and struggle to remain floating as the fight continued. She knew Mecha would win. He was the hero, after all. But for some reason, she was disappointed that she wouldn't be able to watch the conclusion firsthand. Guess she'll just have to read the book…

"Something wrong?"

"No," she shook her head and faced forward again. The bike touched down on the asphalt and continued along the road. "Where are we going now?"

"We'll be leaving this world soon enough." Maître smiled reassuringly. "There's just one last thing I must do, and I'm glad you're here to accompany me for it."

Warmth flooded through her. "Oh? What are we doing?"

"We're going to open this world's Print!" he grinned at her.

"It can be opened?" She tried to remember what he'd told her about the mysterious Prints. "I thought it, like, maintained the world?"

"Yes, but it also serves as a gateway to a space that I've only hypothesized about: the author's Notebook."

"…Right? Okay. What's so special about it?"

"It'll be easier to explain when we get there. You'll see."

She wanted to ask more questions now that they were together again. She wanted to know what he meant when he said that their meddling wouldn't change the outcome of the story, and how time passed here as opposed to the reality, and maybe learn a little more about Maître himself. She wanted to know, but she felt like it wasn't the right time. Especially now, when he seemed so excited, so focused. She'd wait until they were back in the bookshop when things were a little less chaotic, when there was more time to explore her curiosity.

The motorcycle pulled up in front of a building with a colourful sign. Maître's little spider scouts had spun their glowing webs all around the building, giving it a haunted, ethereal vibe. One of the little machines scurried over to its master. Maître crouched down to pick it up and let it crawl along his arm and up to his shoulder. "One of my scouts," he introduced, but Margaret wasn't really listening.

"This is…" She could only stare as the building's glowing letters faded between different colours. 'ARCADE.' "This is Mecha's base."

"You know it?"

"Yeah, I was here earlier," she scowled. "Right after Heinsrick pushed me off a building!" She shook the memory from her head. "You mean to tell me that the Print has been here this whole time?"

"Yes."

He led the way to the door where another spider had just finished spinning a web. Her eyes blurred when she looked at the webbing too closely. She blinked a few times and squinted at the glowing silk. No, it wasn't her eyes; it looked like the webbing itself had a distortion emanating from it, making ripples in the air.

"Uh," she looked over to Maître to point it out, but he was already disappearing inside. Later. She'd ask later.

She stepped into the arcade again and something heavy settled in her chest.

The arcade was still, dark, and quiet except for the dinging of a single game tucked in the back. A lone man played Robo-Slayer: Redemption, tapping away at the buttons and maneuvering the joystick with practiced motions.

"Fatality!"

"Ray?"

The screen turned red as the death screen popped up. "Back so soon?" He looked over his shoulder with a strained smile that fell when he turned his attention to the man in the white coat. "And you found your friend."

Maître stepped forward. "And you found my scouts." He looked at the broken spider robot lying on the console. It was still twitching and sparking. "Yet you're still here."

Ray poked the broken robot. "Not a fan of spiders," he admitted. "And I've got to maintain my title as god of Robo-Slayer." His grin held no humour. "So, what'll it be?"

That heavy thing in her chest started wriggling.

"After all this time, you've stopped hiding." Maître started pacing.

"Hiding? Why would he be hiding?" Margaret asked. This conversation wasn't making any sense. It sounded like they knew each other. She didn't like the atmosphere that had come crashing down on the once lively arcade. "What's going on?" She looked between Ray and Maître.

"He's the Print, my dear," the man in the white coat answered evenly. "The elusive one that has escaped me for so long. Imagine my surprise. I finally regain my freedom, and the first thing I hear is that you've let your guard down."

"I just figured that after years of nothing, you would have forgotten all about this little world," Ray answered. "But it looks like even our guardian won't be coming back." His gaze flicked to Margaret briefly.

She'd thought that nothing else in this world could surprise her. But *Ray* was the Print? She thought it would be, like, a marking on the wall or maybe a magical sigil in the air that was only visible under certain conditions. You know, a physical *print* on the world, not a person. How are you supposed to open a person?

"I—I—" She tried to form a question but didn't know what she was supposed to say.

"It seems this is all moving a little too fast for you, my dear." Maître was suddenly back at her side. "I suppose my explanations have been a bit lax." She looked up at him, wanting to understand. "The Print is the essence of the author—a piece of their soul engraved on the world they created. As such, it takes the form of what the author is most connected to. It can take the form of an object, a location, or even a person."

Margaret turned back to Ray, searching for confirmation. His expression gave nothing away.

Maître continued, "As the Print, he is aware of the true nature of the world he watches over. He knows when someone from outside is interfering. He knows when the story is no longer following the author's design."

"I told you, didn't I?" Ray's smile was forced. "Intuition."

"So…" She tried to pull her thoughts together. "So, when you said I didn't belong here, that my being here was disturbing the universe…"

"I meant it literally. After all, you can't add a new character without altering the original manuscript."

"If you knew everything, why didn't you say so?"

"Because you would have told *him*." Ray glared at Maître. "The team was right. He's the bad guy here."

"Why? Because he teamed up with the villain?"

"No, because he destroyed what this story was supposed to be!"

"What—"

"Now, now," Maître placated, holding up his hands in a calming manner. "You're overexaggerating. Sure, I've meddled here and there—"

"You set it up so that the heroes lose." Ray's voice was ice cold. "You've as good as destroyed the city."

Margaret spun to face Maître. "You said we wouldn't change the story. You said the ending had already been written—that we couldn't change it!"

"Oh, what does it matter anyway?" Maître huffed and rolled his eyes. "There are hundreds of other books with the exact same words and the exact same story out there. What does it matter if one or two copies get bumped off the rails? Makes things a little more interesting."

A door flew open, and a blast of energy shot between them. "Get back!" Gear stepped out from the back room with a giant blaster. His eyes were hard, but his hands were steady.

"Gear..." Margaret couldn't say anything more. There was too much happening too fast.

"So, it turns out I was right about you all along," Gear growled at her. "You *are* with him."

"It's not—" Margaret tried to reason, but Maître stepped in.

"Enough of this," he huffed. His grin was gone. The constant distractions were getting annoying. He pulled out a flat disc the size of a CD and flicked it at Gear like a frisbee. It glowed as it flew, leaving a ghostly silhouette in its path. It cracked into pieces and shot at the boy. Gear dropped the blaster as the pieces pinned him to the wall.

"Knarf!" Gear struggled against the restrains.

"What are you doing!" Margaret yelled at Maître.

"Gear!" Ray tried to help to his cousin, but Maître's hand closed into a fist and the ring on his middle finger sparked to life. The glow shot out towards Ray, encompassed him, and froze him in place.

"Are we all done trying to be heroes?" Maître asked, closing the gap between himself and the Print. Ray struggled against the ring's hold. "Good. Then I'll make this quick."

Maître pulled up his sleeve and revealed his newly designed Portal Generator. It was time to test out its newest feature. He held it out towards Ray, adjusted a few knobs, then pressed the button in the middle. The antenna glowed green, and Maître watched with a mad grin as words started appearing all over Ray's body. The words glowed, then they started to move just like when the Portal Generator created a vortex into a fictional world. Only this time, it was opening over Ray.

In the background, Gear screamed for him to stop, but Ray was beyond words. His entire body glowed, and the portal opened to the author's

Notebook. This portal was different. It wasn't a chaotic vortex, but flat and round like a mirror.

"Marvelous," Maître breathed as he caught his first-ever look inside. He turned back with a smile as bright as the sun and extended his hand to Margaret. "Come along, my dear, and I'll show you something incredible."

Margaret was overwhelmed. What was she supposed to do? What was she supposed to *think*? Through the entire exchange, she hadn't been able to move. She was an outsider stuck watching them.

She looked to Maître's towering form with wide, confused eyes.

What was he doing? How could he do this? These people were... were...

She barely knew these people, but they were good people! Right? Or were they only good because that's how the author wanted them to be? Were they real, or were they just characters?

Her thoughts were a mess. She couldn't think straight. Who was right? Who was wrong? But—

She looked at Maître—the man in the white coat who had a gleam of madness in his eyes. The person who was betrayed by her uncle, someone who had experienced the same pain of being stabbed in the back by a friend. She knew that pain. Had experienced it firsthand.

What Maître was doing right now... it was madness. Could she forgive insanity? Does the end justify the means? What *was* he trying to accomplish? Research for the sake of knowledge? She really didn't know anything beyond that.

She didn't have the whole story. She didn't *know* Maître.

But... he had taken her to *space*! He'd promised her adventure, and by God, she'd gotten it. And this was just the beginning? He had more to show her? Something to make up for all this? Did this man not deserve the benefit of doubt? A chance to explain himself?

She had to choose a side: the heroes that had been taken down so easily, or the man in the white coat who promised her things she'd only *dreamed* of.

She reached out and took his hand.

CHAPTER 12

THE NOTEBOOK

"So, this is it!" Gear spat bitterly as they stepped through the portal. "This is the side you choose? Traitor!"

Traitor!

The accusation hurt. But before she could linger on it, Maître pulled her through the Notebook's mirror-like portal. She felt like Alice stepping through the looking glass. The silver rippled, and green glowed along the edges of her vision as she stepped from one room into the next.

It was quiet. The noise from the arcade disappeared, and she could no longer hear Gear's accusing voice. She looked around and let out a breath as she took in her surroundings. They had stepped into what looked like an amalgamation of many different places. A grassy field with a lone bench morphed into a coffee shop that morphed into a cluttered office that went on and on.

Looking down at herself, she found that she was no longer in her jumpsuit. She had her regular clothes back. The small comfort didn't last long.

"What is this place?" she whispered.

The weight in her chest rolled. This place felt private. It wasn't meant for outsiders. They were intruding here.

"As I thought." Maître was still grinning. He didn't seem to feel the unwelcome weight that Margaret did. His little mechanical spiders scurried around as he spun in place. "It becomes a conglomeration of locations where the actual book was written."

"What?"

"The Notebook is undoubtably the core of each fictional world. And if I'm right, then it also links to every other fictional world created by the same author."

"Seriously?"

"Seriously!" Maître laughed and spread his arms out wide. "After all this time, I'm finally here!"

"So, what's the point of coming here?" Margaret finally asked a question she probably should have asked a long time ago. Her feet moved her toward a desk littered with clutter.

"To learn," Maître answered. "Even as we speak, my scouts are out collecting every scrap of data they can find."

Margaret shuffled some papers around on the desk and found what looked like early character sketches of Mecha and Ringlet. They looked very different from the end result. There were little notes along the margins explaining the design choices and how to link them to other aspects of the story. The weight grew the further she dug.

"I don't think we should stay here." She snatched her hand back to her chest and backed away.

Maître stilled and slowly looked at her. "And why's that?"

"It's just—" She turned to take in the space. She watched as a butterfly settled on the bench, and steam rose from idle cups of coffee. "It's just, it feels like we're intruding here. This isn't meant for us to see."

"Hm…" Maître hummed and watched her. Something about his expression seemed to shift as he rolled her words in his head. "Perhaps you're correct. If you'd prefer, I can finish here by myself. You can wait outside."

"I—" She looked back toward the mirror portal that still glistened. She didn't want to go back there. Not alone.

The glass glinted, and through the mirror she saw something moving. "Heinsrick?"

The villain was supposed to be fighting Mecha in their final showdown. He was singed and seething—his black coat smouldering and his plasma cannons shredded. He locked eyes with Margaret through the glass and he stomped toward the portal. The closer he got, the angrier he became.

Maître turned to face him as the villain leapt through the portal, screaming.

"White Coat!" He aimed what was left of his canons and pulled the trigger.

They exploded, and Margaret screamed as pieces shot around the space, uprooting grass, spilling coffee pots, and sending papers flying. She stared in dismay at the destruction of this intimate space.

In wake of the explosion, Heinsrick stood against Maître. A glistening energy shield had formed in front of Maître and Margaret to block the blast.

"You deadbeat dingo!" Heinsrick screamed. "You set it off early! We were still battling. There was still time! But you set it off and destroyed everything! You thought I wouldn't notice when you slipped in to save your little book keeper? Huh? I had it all figured out! Then you go and blow it all up before schedule!"

"What?" Margaret shook. "What are you talking about?"

"*He* built the Shell of Vengeance," Heinsrick accused, not taking his eyes off Maître. "*He* blew it up! Now everyone's dead!"

Her chest constricted, and she whipped around to stare at Maître. It couldn't... No. She was going to give him a chance to explain. The benefit of doubt. He wasn't...

Was he ruining the story?

"You thought you could get rid of me that easily?" Heinsrick stumbled. He had been beaten, blown up, and burned. He was reaching his limit, but he was still fighting. "Well, you thought wrong!"

"You certainly are persistent," Maître scoffed. He didn't deny it.

"No," she barely managed the words. "Tell me you didn't."

"You really don't know anything, do you?" Heinsrick snarled at her.

"What happens in this world is of no consequence," Maître waved a hand at her.

"What?" She wasn't sure if the word formed properly.

"After all, it's nothing more than words on a page. None of this is real, my dear."

"NO!" she backed away from him. "You're wrong! It's more than words! I hate it when people say that!"

Heinsrick looked between them in confusion but shook it off. "None of that matters." He drew a pocket-sized plasma gun and levelled it at Maître. "The city is ruined. I have no more rivals, my lair is destroyed, my henchmen aren't responding. Everything I've built is gone! The only thing left for me to do is destroy this whole planet and everything on it! Might as well start here."

Two more barrels popped out from the sides of the plasma gun, and it whirred as it powered up. Maître watched on with mild interest as the villain started firing at random, burning through the Notebook. The bench cracked, the tables burned, windows shattered—

A flash. A person materialized from nowhere.

Just as a stray bolt of plasma was about to incinerate the office desk, the faceless person absorbed the shot and vanished as quickly as they appeared, like a whisp that had never been there.

"Interesting," Maître observed. More faceless people rose from the fields and scattered papers. These people were no more than dolls that moved to protect the Notebook's sacred space.

"What is this?" Heinsrick continued to shoot even when the dolls converged on him. The plasma gun was ripped away and the villain was pulled to the ground spitting and hissing.

"That there would be security measures even in here must mean the author was very protective of their work. Well, with how much effort it took to even find this Print, that should be a given. Nevertheless..." Maître pulled out more little discs, the same ones that he'd used against Gear, and in one smooth motion, scattered them around the room. One by one, the dolls were ripped to shreds, but more rose to take their place

A doll reached out for Maître, but the man only grinned.

A spider leapt and attacked. The scouts he had sent out started shooting glowing webs to ensnare the dolls. Seemingly all at once, the dolls fell, tangled in webs, and the discs finished the job.

"What are you doing?" Margaret found her voice. "You ruined the storyline—destroyed the whole city! What are you *really* doing here? What is there to learn from intruding in this private place?"

"My dear, this is the very center of the world." Maître brushed a stray web from his sleeve. His smile faltered when he saw the horror dawning on her face. "Everything is maintained here, this *place* keeps things on track, tries to fix what has deviated from the author's intended purpose. It's how the Print knew you didn't belong here. How it knew that we were disrupting the story. He called it intuition, but it was the Notebook telling him what to do."

"You said we weren't disrupting the story! That we should let it proceed how it was intended to! But *you* were the one messing everything up from the beginning!"

"I figured you would protest, and I had to show you all that we can accomplish."

"And what exactly are we here to accomplish?"

"Well, that Heinsrick fellow was on the right track. We're here to destroy the world."

"What?" she said with a strangled voice.

"This is the epicenter of everything. Destroy the Notebook and the world ceases to exist."

"No." Margaret shook her head, backing away slowly. "No, no, no, no." She was going to let him explain. His explanation was supposed to redeem him! Not—

"Come now, don't be like that," Maître pleaded. "Don't you understand? Once we wipe the Notebook clean, we can create our own world with our own rules!"

"Just write your own goddamn book!" she screamed at him. "Don't go destroying other people's dreams!"

"You know," Maître sighed with a sense of resignation, "you sound just like him."

"Him?"

"Your Uncle Kenneth said the same thing. The hypocrite."

It all clicked into place. "That's why," Margaret breathed. "That's why he locked you in that book! Because you were destroying—oh God. And I *let you out*!"

"Yes. Yes, *you* let me out. I thought I would thank you, show you marvels and wonders that no one else could ever show you."

"I thought you were the good guy."

"Good and bad are relative terms. What's good to one is bad to another."

"Where's the good in erasing an entire world?"

"To build something even better."

"You're willing to *kill* everyone here, all the people who live in this city, because you want to play God?"

"This world may die, but there are thousands more out there—exact copies of the same book in hundreds of other bookstores."

"What does that mean?"

"It means that every copy of *Mecha Arms Fighter: Heinsrick's Vengeance* is another copy of this world. If you miss it so much, just go find another. This version may disappear, but it still exists out there."

"That doesn't justify anything! There are still *lives* being lost."

"But they're not real." He shook his hands, trying to emphasize the point. "They're make-believe. They're characters created by an author with the purpose of entertaining others. They're just *words on a page*."

His words washed over her. How she *hated* those words. Books are more than just stories; she knew that now more than ever. But she had no way of convincing him any more than he could sway her over to his side.

There was no redemption.

They weren't going to understand each other.

She had to stop him.

She'd felt it the moment she stepped through the mirror portal. Her sweater brushing over her arms. The hard plastic belt replaced by comfortable jeans. Then there was the uncomfortable weight that she had stuck into her waistband just before she jumped through the portal into all this madness.

Margaret reached to the small of her back and pulled out the thing she never thought she'd have to use. It seemed like forever ago when she took it from the back room of the Book Portal. At one point, she'd been too scared to even touch it, but she could hardly say that she was scared anymore after facing sharks, spears, and killer robots.

She pulled out her Uncle Ken's old revolver, letting the weight bear down on her soul, and pointed it at Maître.

"Are you sure you want to do this?" The man in the white coat narrowed his eyes.

"I can't let you destroy it." She could feel the emotion spilling into her voice. "I just can't."

"I'm sorry you feel that way." His eyes grew distant and sad.

She didn't allow her hands to tremble as she stared down this man. It wasn't supposed to be like this. It was supposed to be fun adventures, making friends, and trusting someone to have her back. How naïve.

She had come to the Book Portal for a new start. Instead, the betrayal followed her to the other side of the country. Was it even a betrayal if they'd never understood each other to begin with?

It was poetic in a way.

Tears flooded her eyes as she squeezed the trigger.

The bullet exploded from the barrel of the gun.

She didn't see him move.

The energy shield stopped the bullet.

He raised his fist and his glowing ring fired at her.

The green glow trapped her. She couldn't move. She could only watch as he knelt to his case.

His face turned up, and he refused to meet her eye. "I suppose I shouldn't be too surprised that it turned out this way, but I guess we are two very different people. I wish you could have understood. But I can see I won't be able to convince you."

He opened the case and gently lifted out an exact copy of the bomb, the Shell of Vengeance.

Margaret's chest constricted at the sight of it. The first one had taken out half the city. This one would destroy the very essence of this world.

Maître placed it on the ground and it lit up. A twist of a dial and the flick of a few more switches, and the timer flashed on. Thirty seconds until detonation.

He straightened up and turned to her. "Just like your uncle."

She struggled against the restraints as he leaned in close and pulled up her sleeve to reveal the Portal Generator she had found in the secret compartment of her uncle's back room. "You'll be leaving before me," he told her. He still didn't meet her gaze as he set the Generator. The face plate rotated and popped up.

He pressed the face back in and stepped away. The Portal Generator came to life, and he released her from the ring's hold.

She collapsed to the floor, gasping. "Please," she begged as she watched the timer count down on the bomb. "Don't do this."

"I'm sorry, my dear." His back was to her now. "But you wouldn't understand why I need to."

The vortex started forming around her. Her vision was blurred by tears she couldn't stop. Was this really how it was going to end?

A hand gripped her ankle.

She looked down and saw Tidus Heinsrick covered in spider webs, utterly defeated, and clutching at her leg with a mixture of emotions. Anger, frustration, and betrayal flickered across his face, but beyond the façade, she could see his fear.

She didn't stop to think of the consequences. She met his reach. Their eyes locked, and an understanding passed between them. With what strength she had left, she gathered the young villain close and held him as the vortex encompassed them both.

Wind ripped at her clothes and threatened to tear her away from Heinsrick. She held on tighter and buried her face into his hair.

Then it was quiet.

She opened her eyes. They were back in the Book Portal. Tucked in behind the counter. The book was laid out in front of them.

For a long while, she just sat there, unable to move. Heinsrick hadn't been able to stay conscious and was passed out against her. She gently laid him down on the floor.

It didn't feel real, looking around at her little bookshop. She spent so much time getting it all cleaned, organized, and ready to open. None of it seemed to matter anymore.

She looked at the book, *Mecha Arms Fighter: Heinsrick's Vengeance*. She reached out to the book, but her fingers could only hover above the pages.

Did they really alter the story? Did they physically change the words in the book? How far did their meddling really go?

Then it happened.

The words on the pages started bleeding. She snatched her hand back. The ink spilled from the letters like they were crying, staining each page blacker and blacker until there was nothing but darkness left.

It was gone. Just like that, the words on the page drowned in a sea of ink. An entire world snuffed out.

She bit back a sob and threw the book across the room in frustration before breaking down. She pulled her knees up to her chest and pulled at her hair as she sobbed over the people she'd met, the places she'd been, the things she'd seen.

Mecha, Ringlet, and Gear. The members of H². The people just walking down the street…

Ray.

All gone.

Nothing but black, unreadable pages.

The only thing left was…

Tidus Heinsrick. He lay beside her. His eyes were closed, but his chest was still rising and falling with even breaths. He was still singed, still covered in cobwebs, but he was breathing. He was alive.

The only one left is the villain, she thought ironically, placing a protective hand on his forehead. He scrunched his brow at the contact but didn't wake up. *There's gotta be some philosophical meaning to that.* But she didn't want to think about that right now.

She wiped her hands down her face and scrubbed at her eyes with the back of her arm. Bracing herself on the counter, she hauled herself up because this wasn't done.

He still had to come *out.*

Sure enough, the book she had thrown across the room snapped open. There were no words to form a vortex this time. The pages themselves fluttered, and the black ink that stained them rose in a dark vortex of nothing. The wind whipped around the shop, and after a dramatic moment, Maître stepped out of the ruined world and back into reality.

The portal closed behind him, and silence took over as they stared at each other. He had the decency to look ashamed, but she suspected it was more disappointment than regret.

"What now?" She broke the silence.

"That's what I should be asking," he answered.

"Don't play your little word games with me," she growled.

He sighed in defeat. "If you want to know whether I'm finished or not, then no. I'm only just beginning."

"I can't let you keep doing this."

"Then you'll just have to try and stop me." He smiled weakly.

"Then I will. With everything I have."

He took a moment to really look at the girl again. He ran his eyes along her ridged form, her tear-stained face, the determination etched into her stare. "It's interesting," he chuckled.

"What is?"

"The name you gave me. Maître. *The Master.*"

She glared at him, and her cheeks burned with embarrassment from her naïve fangirl way of thinking.

He nodded and continued, "Then let me give you one also. From now on, you'll be the Guardian of Books. The Book Keeper. Protect them for as long as you can." The mischievous look returned to his eyes with the sadness expertly masked. "But I won't make it easy." His tone shifted quickly. Gone was the gloom and melancholy, replaced by an easy challenge. She didn't miss the weight that still sat heavy on his shoulders. He may be free of his Greek prison, but he was still alone.

He turned and retrieved something from his coat pocket. He turned it over in his hands, eyeing the little mechanisms and the details he'd put together himself. "We could have made a great duo, you and I," he said softly and placed the little mechanical sparrow on one of the bookshelves. "But I suppose I'll just have to settle for a new rivalry."

His back straightened, and he glanced over his shoulder to look at her out of the corner of his eye as a new portal started opening. "May we clash again, Book Keeper."

"Count on it, Maître," she answered his challenge and watched as he disappeared into an unknown book on the shelf.

"That's it? You're just letting him go?" A strained voice at her feet startled her. Tidus Heinsrick managed to prop himself up against the wall with shaky arms.

She let out a breath of relief and crouched down beside him. "How and I supposed to stop him as I am now?"

Heinsrick grit his teeth and smashed a fist into the floor. "Damnit! How could I have lost so badly? And to *him*! The only one allowed to defeat me is Mecha." He hung his head and cradled his hands in his lap.

She didn't know what to do. Didn't know how to comfort him.

"It's gone, isn't it?" he asked, voice little more than a whisper. "My entire world is gone?"

She nodded silently and felt something rip open in her chest at his words.

"And that dillweed is going to keep doing it?"

She nodded again.

"Then I guess there's only one thing to do."

She tilted her head in silent query.

"I'm going to destroy him."

She facepalmed hard. "Seriously?" she asked, exasperated. "You're gonna go the revenge route?"

"Revenge? That's not what this is about." Heinsrick looked at her incredulously. The sorrow and weight of losing his home was surprisingly absent. "This is a matter of pride! *I* was supposed to destroy the world, and he beat me to it! I will destroy him for it!"

"And after that?" she asked cautiously. "Are you gonna start trying to destroy this world?"

"Haven't decided yet." He stretched his arms above his head and stood up. His injuries, which had seemed bad before, were now nothing more than an afterthought. "I said it before, but I don't have anything against your world. So, you're off the hook for now. I'll decide what'll happen next *after* we defeat White Coat."

"And until then?"

He looked down at her, still crouched on the floor. "I guess we're working together until further notice."

She smiled up at him. Sure, he was a villain and a goof obsessed with plasma, but he could have been worse. "Alright, then." She stood up and offered a hand to him. "Partners, then?"

He looked at her critically. "I'd prefer henchman, but I suppose we can be equals."

"Oh, really?" She raised her eyebrows.

"Is there a problem?"

"I suppose not."

The bells from the front of the shop rang. A man in a navy t-shirt and jeans peeked in. "Delivery. I have the couches you ordered."

"Oh." She looked at him, then around at the shop with the realization that she still had real-life responsibilities. "I thought they weren't coming until tomorrow…"

"Did you want us to come back?" He gestured to the truck parked out front.

"No, no, it's okay," she waved him in. "I've got the space cleared already."

The man nodded and went to help his co-worker lift the new couches out of the van.

"What's happening?" Heinsrick leaned in and asked.

She looked back at him, then out the front door. "I'm opening a bookshop."

CPSIA information can be obtained
at www.ICGtesting.com
Printed in the USA
BVHW051720151022
649212BV00001BA/52